MW01138889

Remembrance

T.K. Eldridge

Graffridge Publishing

Contents

To my great-grandmother, Hazel Pearl Roberts Reynolds, for always encouraging me, for buying me my first electric typewriter - and for reminding me to live with no regrets.

To my parents, Charles & Elizabeth Eldridge, for always believing in me and knowing that I would, some day, achieve this dream

"Revenge is an act of passion, vengeance is the act of justice." - Samuel Johnson

Remembrance: Prologue

Camille Brewster shifted the weight of her sleeping daughter in her arms and tucked the crocheted blanket around Emmy a little more securely. Times like this were when she realized that she'd made the right decision to move from Boston and settle on Cape Cod. A quiet town, Muckle Cove had a good school system and a solid sense of community.

Simple things she hadn't realized were valuable until six months ago when it had all come crashing down. Back then, the only thing holding her to Boston was a job she had grown to despise. Being a fashion writer had been her dream for as long as she could remember and writing for Harper's had been a realization of that dream - until Emlen was born.

Funny how having a child completely changed one's priorities.

Her mind skimmed over the past few years. Meeting JJ at the gala - their whirlwind relationship and the bitter crash at the end. Her realization that this child would be hers and hers alone. All of it had brought her to this place and this point in time. Cradling this sweet little girl in her arms, listening to her soft breaths mingling with the pounding of waves on the beach still audible even through the closed windows. A sense of contentment washed over her as Cami let herself drift into near sleep. She'd make this life work for them - peace, security and stability.

The creak of the floor in the back hallway is what must've woken her, but for a few moments, Cami couldn't figure out what had brought her suddenly awake. The faint gleam of the light over the sink in the kitchen and the dim lamp in the living room where she sat were the only illumination in the house. Barely breathing, she listened intently to the house and her sleeping child, wondering what had her trembling in anticipation. Again, a soft shuffle of a shoe in the hall and Cami knew someone was in her house. Rising slowly from the rocker, she moved to the built-in blanket chest under the window and carefully lifted the lid before moving to place Emmy in the niche. The child's eyes opened wide and Cami pressed a finger to the girl's lips.

"Shh. Stay quiet and don't come out, no matter what, until I get you, okay?"

A faint nod from Emmy and Cami slowly lowered the lid, the mesh vent in the front of the chest allowing plenty of air into the space.

Cami reached for the fireplace poker, a faint scrape of metal sounding much too loud as she armed herself against the intruder. Hefting it like a baseball bat, she stepped towards the hallway and waited just out of sight.

One breath...two...and she saw a gloved hand holding a revolver slip past the edge of the wall. Bringing the poker down hard, she heard a man's cry of pain and the roar and flash of a bullet hitting the hardwood floor a few feet away. Suddenly fear that Emlen would accidentally get shot had her moving to swing again, but the man had turned the corner and the gun was coming up towards her. A face she vaguely recognized met her wide eyes before she heard the sound of the gun firing once more, a sharp spike of pain at the side of her head, and everything went dark.

Cursing, the man grabbed his forearm, pretty sure the blow she'd dealt him had broken it. Looking at the woman's body sprawled on the floor, the growing puddle of blood under her head, he kicked the poker out of the way and leaned down to listen. No breathing. Good. Picking up the fireplace tool, he placed it back in the stand and glanced around the room.

"Now to find the brat." He muttered as he turned towards the bedrooms.

Looking first in one room, then the other, he didn't see any sign of the child. "Bloody hell." He cursed as he pulled out his radio, thumbing the button. "She's down. Kid isn't here."

"Of course she's there. Keep looking!" the voice yelled back at him.

"No, really, she's not here. Maybe she's at the aunt's or something?" the shooter replied.

A few minutes hesitation and then a low growl. "Fine. Get out. I'll deal with your fuck up later."

Another look around the room and the man turned, heading back out the way he came, gloves leaving no fingerprints, revolver leaving no casings, just a faint click as he closed the door.

Silence filled the small cottage. It was probably close to an hour before Emlen pushed the lid up on her hiding spot and crawled out. "Mummy?" she whispered, pajama covered feet padding closer to the still figure on the floor. A tiny hand reached out to pat Cami's still face. "Mummy? I waited. Wake up, Mummy." When Cami didn't stir, Emlen sighed and curled up against her mother's side, head resting on her mother's belly where she fell asleep.

———◦———

James O'Brien parked his pickup in the gravel drive outside the cottage and set his travel mug in the console holder. Glancing at the work order, he went over it one more time before he stepped out and reached into the back to grab his toolbox. This job had been scheduled for about a week and it didn't look like it was going to take him long. Repairing the railing on the porch and fixing the pantry door - could be easy or could turn into one of those jobs where starting to fix one thing opened up a whole 'nother mess of problems.

He'd spoken to Camille Brewster two days ago to verify the appointment time and stepped up to the door where his knuckles rapped next to the glass panes with a brisk tap. He waited a few moments, then knocked again. He cupped his hand against the glass and James peered in through the lace curtains hanging over the door window. "Ms. Brewster?" he called out and then caught his breath as he saw a small girl walking towards him. She looked like she'd been playing with paints and was trailing bits of cereal from the box she hugged against her chest.

"Mummy's sleepin' on the floor." the child called out and the first stirrings of panic whirled in James' chest.

He reached for the doorknob and twisted. Unlocked, the door opened easily. He looked into the hallway and shouted "Ms. Brewster? It's James O'Brien. Are you okay?"

"Mummy's there." The little girl said and pointed towards the living room.

James took a couple of steps inside and the smell hit him first before he noticed a pair of white sock-covered feet sprawled just inside the living room archway. He fumbled in his pocket before he flipped his phone open and dialed 911. It only took him a few words to get the operator to send help, and her insistence he stay on the line was ignored as he turned to look at the child once more. What he had thought was paint he was pretty sure now was blood.

Crouching down, he smiled at the child. "What's your name, honey?" he asked softly.

"I'm Emmy." She replied. "I'm three and a half." She held up three fingers and smiled. "I'll be four at Christmas."

He turned to his right, to the bathroom, then reached in and grabbed a bath towel before James scooped up the child, careful to not get any of the blood on himself. Wrapping her up, he headed back out to his truck, the door to the house pulled closed behind him. A moment later, he set the child on the truck's bench seat. "Are you thirsty?" he asked and pulled a bottle of water out of his lunch cooler, then opened it up and handed it to her.

Red smeared the plastic as she gripped the wet bottle and drank about a third before she gasped and smiled up at him. "Fank you. I drinked all the juice all gone."

All James could think about were his own two boys, only a couple of years older than this little one. He grabbed a couple of wet wipes to clean her hands and face, then tucked them into a plastic trash bag in case the police needed them. He pulled his lunch towards him and looked up at Emlen. "Hungry? I've got a ham and cheese sandwich, some carrots and a couple of cookies." Being a normal child, she of course reached for the cookies and James let her. As she munched away between sips of water, the sounds of sirens slowly grew louder before shutting off as a town cruiser pulled up. "You stay right here, and I'll be back. I'm just going to talk to the nice policeman, okay?"

Emlen nodded, her attention on the cookies as James closed the truck door, pocketing his keys as he headed over to the sheriff. "Hey Joel, thanks for getting here so quick. It looks real bad. I've got the little one in my truck, wrapped in a bath towel, but she's covered in blood and none of it her own."

Joel Desantis, sheriff in Muckle Cove for the past eighteen years, ran a hand over his bald head before settling his cap in place and nodded to James' words. "Let me go take a look and then we'll talk. Do you know if she's got family in the area or anything? Someone to take care of the kid?"

"She's got some family in Hyannisport and some in Boston, from what I could gather the few times we've chatted. I've been coming by for the past few months, slowly fixing things on the cottage. She kept a big address book on the shelf next to the phone in the kitchen, so maybe there's something in there. I didn't touch anything but the towel and the child after I stepped inside. Even saved the wet wipes I cleaned her hands and face with, in case you need them," James replied. "If you need me to take the girl home, Eileen and I can keep an eye on her until you contact family."

Joel nodded. "Let me take a look first and I'll get back to you on that."

Joel turned away from James and headed up to the house. He slowed as he peered into the truck at the little girl wrapped in a towel, eating a cookie. She didn't notice him as he kept on walking and stepped inside.

As with James, the smell told Joel that Camille Brewster was dead. A quick canvass of the scene and Joel went into the child's room to grab a change of clothes and a stuffed toy off the bed before he found the aforementioned address book in kitchen. He paused and leaned over the body, gently taking a necklace off Camille. In the bathroom he rinsed the blood from the roughly inch long amber egg wrapped in silver vines, then dried it and tucked it into the zipper back of the stuffed bunny.

It was the best he could do to keep the gem close to Emlen. It had to be close to her. Once outside, he jogged over to his car to collect the crime scene tape with one hand, dialing his phone with the other. "This is Sheriff Desantis over in Muckle Cove. I need state CSI and investigators at 15 Rocky Ridge, ASAP."

Hours later, Emlen was bathed and fed and changed, curled up asleep in Eileen O'Brien's arms, bunny hugged tight. The bloody clothes had been bagged and tagged, and once CSI was done with the house, Joel had brought Eileen into the child's room to pack her a bag to last a few days.

It had taken nearly six hours to get ahold of her family, but no one was rushing to claim the girl, so she was with James and Eileen for now.

Muckle Cove didn't have a dedicated CPS office. The town was small enough that it was not uncommon for kids in need to stay with a local family until processing could be done.

Glancing down at the sleeping child in her arms, Eileen rocked gently as she spoke to James seated nearby. "What do you think will happen to her?"

"Her family will come get her, I guess." His voice sounded weary and yet he couldn't take his eyes off the little girl curled against his wife. "Joel was pretty pissed though. Seems like no one really wants her. Something about Camille not being married and the child having no known father."

Eileen made a rude noise and her gaze flashed to James "Are you serious right now? It's...what...nearly the twenty-first century and they're worried about legitimacy?"

"Remember, Eileen, they're from money. Stuff like that matters to them, I guess." James leaned back, taking a sip of coffee. "I'll never forget what I saw today," he whispered low. "Made me want to do nothing more than just hug Cullen and Connor."

Eileen started to ask what he'd really seen, but when James' gaze settled on hers, she stopped mid statement and sighed. His eyes were positively haunted. "It's not us. We're all fine. But I'd appreciate it if you'd be home before dark for the next few nights until they catch whoever did that." A nod from him and Eileen rose with the sleeping child. "I'll put her on the cot in our room so I can keep an eye on her tonight. Come up soon, okay?"

James rose too and kissed her cheek as she moved past before he went to secure the house - again - for the night.

Emlen had seen the files from the case, but she didn't remember much of the actual events. In fact, she really had no clear memories at all until a year after the murder. Her grandparents had refused to take her in until her aunt Corinne had guilted them into retrieving her, yet it was still nearly six months later that she left the O'Brien's home. She had a feeling of affection and safety when she thought of the O'Briens, but no actual visual memory. Everything she knew as facts all came from records. The files stated Joseph and Emilia Brewster had sent the O'Brien family money for her care and signed temporary guardianship over to them. It was thought, for a time, that they would be able to adopt the little girl.

News stories kept the murder from completely fading from sight, finding new fodder each time someone was brought in for questioning. It was when James O'Brien himself was questioned that things got really messy. Did the society couple of the senior Brewster's leave their granddaughter with a murderer? Did Corinne, wife of Jonathan Hale and mother to the heir to the Hale fortune, leave her only sister's child in the hands of the man that was a likely killer?

The media crucified James O'Brien, even when zero evidence was found against him. Corinne and Jonathan obtained guardianship of Emlen and within a year, the child was put in her first boarding school.

James and Eileen took the boys and moved out of state for nearly five years before they returned in time for both sons to attend, and graduate from Cove High.

Over two decades had passed - and no murderer was ever found.

2

Remembrance: Chapter One

Emlen stepped up to the porch that ran along the front of the General Store and flashed her fake press pass to the group of ladies sitting around a rough wooden table - coffee cups and cards scattered across the surface. "Good afternoon, ladies. I'm here from the New York Transcript and would like to speak with you."

Well, that wasn't a full out lie. Emlen did plan on selling the story to any number of outlets, including the New York Transcript, but she hadn't been a stringer for them in a few years. As far as Emlen was concerned, 'any means necessary' went a long way when you were digging for a story.

"Is it about the road repair project over near the bridge?" one woman asked, her salt-and-pepper curls bouncing as she looked up at Emlen.

"They're taking way too long with that. I can't stand the smell of hot tar when I'm out trying to tend my gardens."

"Oh, Martha, why would a New York paper care about a local road project?" another replied as she rose from her seat, she offered her hand. "Janet Martin. A pleasure to meet you, miss. What questions do you have?"

Emlen shook Janet's hand and smiled at the woman. A braided crown of pure white wrapped around Janet's head and clear blue eyes glinted with intelligence as she gestured to a seat for Emlen, then nodded to the carafe of coffee and stack of mugs on the table. "Would you like a coffee?"

"Yes, thank you. I'm Emilia Baldwin and I'm doing a follow up story on something that happened in Muckle Cove about twenty years ago." Emlen took her seat, set her phone on the table and glanced around. "Do you mind if I record this conversation? Helps with my notes." After a chorus of "go ahead" and "no problem", she clicked the record app on her phone and accepted a mug of coffee. "First, I'd like your names, please?"

Janet Martin, the apparent ringleader, spoke up first, followed by Martha Riggs, Susan Clark and Jessica Sanford. A few people came up the steps and passed into the store or on the way out, a couple of glances cast their way, but no one interfered.

"Are you talking about the Brewster murder?" Janet asked, eyes brightening. It was clear that gossip was her stock in trade, and she leaned forward, radiating excitement that could only be related to speaking about the worst thing to happen in their little coastal town in decades. "I spoke to Camille a few times when she was out shopping or walking with that beautiful baby of hers. It's a real shame what happened to them."

"Actually, yes, Mrs. Martin, that is why I'm here. It's coming up on twenty years since the murder and I'm doing a piece about it."

A gust of wind swirled by and the sweet scent of vanilla musk was so strong, Emlen could almost taste it, her eyes drifting closed for a moment at the fragments of memory it stirred. A quick breath and Emlen slapped the smile back on her face and looked at the women in front of her. "So, were all of you residents of Muckle Cove at the time of the murder?"

They all nodded.

After a sip of her coffee, Jessica Sanford sighed. "My husband, Eddie and I moved here about three days after it happened. I wanted to move right back out, but we couldn't afford it."

Martha reached over and rested a hand over Jessica's. "That's how we met. I lived two houses down from Jess and Eddie. We'd stay at her house or mine, together with the kids, while the guys went out. Commercial fishing. They would have to leave at three in the morning to get out on the water. We just felt better being together instead of a woman alone with little ones in the house."

Fingers wrapped around her bright red mug, Emlen took a sip of coffee and let the women talk. Another one of those trade secrets she learned early - get the ball rolling and let them spill. Nudge the ball back on track if it went too far off course, yet you never knew what kind of info that 'off course' might bring out.

Truth, for her, was easy to spot. It was in the words spoken, the expressions on a face, the body language and gestures. One of her friends had said that it was uncanny how accurate Emlen was when it came to sussing out liars. Big lies, little lies, it didn't matter. She could tell. Eh, some people were good at math, Em was good at reading people.

Susan had been quiet the longest as she picked at the Danish remains on her plate.

Emlen turned her gaze to the tiny woman. Once dark hair, liberally streaked with gray, cut in a short style that was both youthful and flattering. A crisp peach cotton top and a pair of olive-green capris with matching slip on canvas shoes - her look spoke of both comfort and style. Small gold hoops in her ears, gold chain with a pendant that had slipped inside her shirt, a bangle bracelet, slim gold watch and three or four rings on her hands completed the picture.

The weight of Emlen's stare must have finally registered because Susan's gaze lifted to meet hers. "It was my fault," she finally whispered softly as the other women fell silent.

Eyes widening, Emlen set down her cup and blinked at the woman. "Your fault? How do you figure?"

"I was supposed to go by the night it happened. I had some books Cami wanted to borrow, and she had some for me - but it was so stormy, I called to reschedule for a few days later. If I had been there..." Susan's voice caught and she pressed her fingers to her lips, looking down.

Janet reached over and rested a hand on Susan's shoulder. "If you had been there, he might have killed you too. This is not on you, Susie - it's on him, the murdering bastard who killed her and ruined that little girl's life."

It took Emlen a few moments to process what had been said before she murmured, "The little girl went to her aunt and uncle and was okay." No, not a great life, but a tolerable one. Mostly. She shook her head as if clearing a fog and smiled at Susan. "Janet is right. He probably would have killed you too. None of it is on you." The words sounded perfectly sincere, but Em couldn't help but agree with Susan - that if she had been there, then maybe her mother wouldn't have been murdered after all.

A softly whispered, "Maybe..." came from Susan as she dug in her purse for a tissue and wiped her eyes. "I'm sorry, I should go." She rose from her seat and hurried away before the others could get more than a "...no, don't..." out of their mouths.

Janet's shoulders sagged. "She's been carrying that for twenty years, poor thing." Slim fingers fiddled with her coffee cup. "This whole town changed a bit that day. Oh, sure, other 'bad things' have happened over the years, but that one shook the foundations of the community. People still talk about it, now and again. I guess that's because it's still unsolved. A cold case is what they call it, right?" Janet glanced up at Emlen and gave her a faint smile.

"Yes, that's correct. It is still an open case, but inactive at this point. No one expects to find new evidence or clues at this stage of the game," Em replied, starting to gather her things. "I'm sorry my questions upset Susan. I hope the rest of you didn't mind too much?" She pasted the perfectly professional smile back on her face.

Personally? She really didn't care that Susan had become upset. It gave her so much information and opportunity. Clearly there was more going on there. Susan was lying about something related to her mother, and with her being so upset, Em could stop by Susan's house later with the excuse of 'checking on her' and 'apologizing for upsetting her' while actually getting an opportunity to speak with the woman alone. Alone, without the scrutiny or support of her friends, Susan might be a bit more forthcoming.

A few head shakes from the remaining ladies and Jessica excused herself. "I should make sure Susan gets home okay. Lovely to meet you, Ms. Baldwin." She hurried off, leaving Martha and Janet to stack up the cups and serving plate and leave a tip for the counter girl who cleaned up.

Emlen checked her notes and phone, then tucked them away before she pulled out cards she'd printed up with her fake name, cell number and email address. "If you think of anything else or if the others do and want to share, please call or email me?" Again, Em felt that perfect smile grace her lips. She lay the cards on the table before she headed back to her car.

She climbed in, bag on the passenger's seat floor, then Emlen set her phone in the holder and leaned back, taking a couple of slow breaths and processing what she'd heard. Again, that scent of vanilla musk swirled past and she sat up, looking around to see if someone was standing near.

No one was remotely close to her parking spot and she couldn't quite place that scent. It was familiar and comforting - but where was it coming from? She took a breath to clear her head, then Emlen started the vehicle and headed out.

She'd stopped earlier to drop her bags, but it was time to head to the cottage and settle in. She'd worry about Susan later.

Maybe.

3

Remembrance: Chapter Two

After so many years, it surprised Emlen how much felt familiar as she drove through Muckle Cove. She'd lived here with her mother for less than a year when she was a toddler. She'd only been back maybe two other times for day trips with her uncle, to handle paperwork or business related to the cottage property. The Cove was a typical New England coastal town that hugged the inner harbor of Cape Cod. Widow's walks and fanciful weathervanes topped the weathered shingle houses and brick antiquities.

She'd always wondered why her mother came here, of all places. The only thing Emlen could think of was that it was as close to her roots she could get. Camille Eugenie Brewster, great-great however-many granddaughter of Elder William Brewster from the Mayflower, had run from Boston and New York and that lifestyle to find herself settled here with a baby in the middle of nowhere.

As she pulled up in front of the cottage, Emlen shut off the vehicle and gathered her things before she took a moment to just look at the place. Stone foundation topped with a gray weathered clapboard house of a story and a half. Modest, as far as her family's other homes were concerned, but perfect for her.

Two bedrooms and a bath, a large eat-in kitchen and a living room with a fireplace that was split with glass doors so one half could be used as a study. Trimmed in white with a colonial blue door, stone steps leading up to the door had enough room on either side for potted plants. Once inside, the hallway led to the back of the house where the kitchen and living room shared a wall of glass, framing a view of the back deck and the harbor beyond. Off the kitchen, narrow stairs led to a locked door to the attic with windows on either end and dormer windows on front and back.

Sea roses climbed a trellis outside the window over the kitchen sink, a blush pink with a scent that could fill the house with the slightest breeze.

For years, the cottage had been rented to summer tenants. No one stayed there long.

No one could.

Families that rented the pretty beach cottage often reported the desperate crying of a child that seemed to come at different times. The poor vacationers rarely shared the stories of a panicked woman's screams that would shatter the sunny afternoons, ending with them grabbing their belongings and tearing down the dirt road, dust flying.

The last group left just two days before, saving Em the trouble of having to evict them. She hadn't planned on coming to Muckle Cove at all, really. Not consciously, anyway. Subconsciously, oh, she probably knew she would end up here for the last six months, maybe a year.

Crouched near the bottom of the stone steps, Emlen found a pretty scallop shell that some seeker of beach treasures must've dropped. Her thumb idly rubbed the sand from the pale peach interior while her gaze tracked the high tide hiss and grasp at the shore a hundred yards away. Again, Em wondered why she was here. Then again, why does anyone seek roots?

Why would they want to look back into the past before stepping forward into the future?

Emlen had little to nothing to say in regard to that. She'd left Brad holding the ring and climbed in her car. Bradley Wallingford Smith, V. The fifth. Four others with the same pretentious name...and the same propensity for making money as if it were collecting shells on the beach.

Her Aunt Cassie bemoaned the potentially 'lost' marriage as if it were a winning lottery ticket someone misplaced. Uncle Nelson thought Emlen was doing the right thing and taking a moment to make sure this was what she wanted. Before. Before she got married. Before she made those choices. Before she sealed her fate.

A shrug of her shoulders and Emlen rose to her feet, then tucked the shell into her pocket. She stepped up to the Victorian style wooden screen door and pulled it open, then let it slap noisily shut behind her when she entered the shadowed cottage.

The layout hadn't changed. The sofa and chairs were new. The kitchen set replaced. Paint. Paper. Appliances. It had been twenty years, give or take a few months, and upkeep and updating must be done.

Ownership of the cottage, and her trust fund, had been transferred to her upon her eighteenth birthday. Emlen had dutifully paid her uncle's management company to keep up with the needed repairs and maintenance. She had planned on selling it – but never quite could.

Perhaps, somehow, she had known she would need it some day?

Fumbling with the keys in her pocket, Emlen moved toward the door near the back, off the kitchen. The attic was kept locked to keep tenants from poking into the things stored up there. The stiff lock screeched as Emlen turned it. No one had been in it since workmen had replaced the roof ten years ago. Opening the door, a haze of dust drifted past, bringing a series of sneezes and coughs before she could stare up the stairs through tearing eyes. Light streamed through the window in the back peak of the roof and for a moment, Emlen could swear she saw someone pass by as a shadow slid halfway down the stairs. She shivered and stepped back, closing the door. "Maybe tomorrow," Emlen whispered, locking it once more.

The place felt smaller than she remembered – that oddity that happens to all who go back to somewhere they only have childhood memories of, that skews one's sense of perception. Em turned on lights and drew the curtains back then opened the windows wide to let in the smell of salt and sea and chase the aroma of dust and suntan lotion away.

Simple tasks of mundane processing that are the first steps to making a space one's own. Windows open to cleanse the room of scents that were not one's own. Little steps, like setting out a favored mug on the counter for coffee and rearranging the utensils in the drawers so they were familiar. Convenient.

She placed the little shell from her pocket on the counter between the kitchen island and the living room, beside a stone and a bit of sea glass someone else had collected and displayed. Emlen smiled at the glint of sunlight on the opaque green bit of treasure and started to hum a bright tune as she tugged her duffel into the larger bedroom, drawing her slippers and bathrobe out of it to place by the bed and on the hook on the bathroom door. She arranged her toiletries neatly on the shelves over the sink. Slowly, she made this place hers, although right now there was nothing that felt of home to her. No more than her dormitory or any number of hotel rooms had been over the years.

If any place was going to be home to her, this one should be it – as this is where she lived the longest with family. Granted, the dorm at Emerson Preparatory had been her residence for nearly seven years – one failed roommate experience before a series of private rooms, it had been where she spent most of her time. But how much 'home' could one make out of a public facility?

The four years at Harvard hadn't done it for her either. There had been three different apartments before finding a studio on her own.

Em lined the drawers of the Shaker style wooden dresser with lavender paper, then laid her clothes inside and finally emptied the duffel bag.

"Might as well go all the way. In for a penny..." her voice trailed off as she slid the last drawer closed and looked around the room. More comfortable than any dorm room, more personable than any hotel room, and slowly it started to feel like hers.

A plaintive meowing startled her out of her thoughts and Emlen headed into the main room to see a small gray cat at the back screen door. "Well, that helps. I'd rather be thought strange for talking to a pet than to myself." Opening the door, she clucked her tongue and urged the cat inside. "Come on in, shadow-cat. I think I saw a can of cat food here somewhere."

Padding into the kitchen, Emlen followed the cat who seemed to know as well as she did, if not better, where a can of cat food was stored.

"I see you're familiar with the territory. Fine. I'll do the can opener for you this time though, all right? You guys ever figure them out, we humans are toast." Laughing at herself, Emlen dumped the food out onto a chipped saucer and set it down for the feline. "No collar. Everyone has to have a name, eh, shadow-cat?" Emlen continued her discourse with her aloof dining companion as she heated up a can of soup and opened a package of crackers, leaning against the granite countertops and sipping the soup from an oversized mug, watching the cat devour the food. "You look like a Barnabas."

The cat paused to look up at her and lick his whiskers clean. "You like that name? Barnabas? Fine. Then Barnabas it is." Emlen decreed and laughed as the cat sneezed and returned to eating. "No editorial comments from the peanut gallery, m'friend."

The discourse with her new 'roommate' was interrupted by a tap on the door. The golden wash of afternoon sunshine was behind the person standing there, so, once again, all Emlen saw was a shadow at her door. A flicker of a memory skittered in the deep recesses of her mind before she shook it off and set the soup down on the counter.

"Pardon, ma'am, but Jake up at the store said you had an order to be delivered and while you might not be expecting it until tomorrow, I told him I'd bring it by on my way." The voice was a near-purr of a baritone and the shadowy form slowly coalesced into a rather prime example of American male the closer Emlen walked to the door. Prime male, holding a large cardboard box piled high with grocery bags.

"Well, talk about service!" Emlen smiled, unlocking the screen, letting the man in. As he passed, she couldn't help but notice he also smelled male. That faintly spicy whiff of after shave layered over a touch of sweat and the laundry soap used on his clothes. The curl of his dark hair where it brushed the collar of his shirt, the way the blue of the chamois brought out the color of his eyes - the way his jeans tightened as he bent to set the box on the table. With a little shake, Emlen stopped staring and grinned wryly, holding out her hand as soon as his are empty. "Emmy B...Baldwin. Thank you, Mister...." Her voice trailed off and his obligingly filled in.

"Cullen O'Brien, Miz Baldwin." He answered as his hand wrapped around hers and shook it firmly. "But you can call me Cullen." His eyes traced over her form and then settled again on her face. "Might I say, Miz Baldwin, you've got the most unusual eyes I've ever seen."

Emlen's heart froze for a moment, then she realized she still had the contact lenses in and let out a slow breath. "Thank you." The gray-hued lenses did give her unusual eyes. "Good genetics."

Cullen gave her a slow smile, apparently doing his best to keep the once-over a touch more subtle than obvious. "Yes, ma'am. Very good genetics."

Even white teeth. Gods, he even had a dimple in his cheek. Emlen once again caught herself staring and pressed a hand to her belly to quiet the slowly coiling heat that had started up there. "Well..." Emlen reached for her purse on the counter and began to pull out her wallet, nearly knocking over the radio. Do I have any cash? I can't let him see my license. Five bucks...

"No, ma'am, I don't need any money. It was on my way. I live in the next house down the beach. You can see it from your porch if you lean out a bit, or just look out the windows on that side." Cullen's voice trailed off and he shrugged, a shy grin teasing that dimple out of his cheek. "If you need anything, I'd be more than happy to stop by. I helped the maintenance crew do some of the repairs last summer."

Em's thoughts went to 'I bet he looks great in a tool belt. And nothing else.' "Umm, sure. I've noticed a couple of things I'd like to get seen to. I'll give you a call in a few days once I get settled. Do you have a card?" Emlen asked when what she wanted to ask was 'Do you have a girlfriend or wife?'.

Cullen reached into his pocket and pulled out a pen, shaking his head. "No, no card." He stepped back to the box on the table and tore a scrap from one of the bags, writing his number on it and handing it to Emlen. "Here ya go. Give me a call when you're ready."

"Okay. Well, thank you again. Bye!" Emlen waved and watched him head back out to his truck. Scratched and faded, the old Ford starting up with a roar, tires spitting gravel and sand as he turned around and drove away.

A soft mrowl as the cat twined around her ankles and Emlen chuckled. "Well, a tom cat and a hottie all in one day. How lucky can a girl get, eh Barnabus?"

Gloria Estefan's "Miami Sound Machine" and the spicy Salsa beat poured from the radio as she turned it up. It kept Emlen moving. She unpacked and put away the groceries, wiped down shelves and lined them with fresh paper, cleaned dishes and arranged the kitchen the way she liked it. Within a couple of hours, she was done. The sunlight had long since faded and the lamps glowed warm and golden yellow in the summer darkness.

4

Remembrance: Chapter Three

Emlen let Barnabus out and locked the door, leaving one small light on over the stove and shut off the rest as she wandered through to the bathroom. She started the bathtub to fill for a good long soak before checking the locks one last time.

She sank into the steaming water, grateful that the claw foot tub gave her enough space to really relax. Mentally, Emlen went back over her day. There was the strangeness of coming back to Muckle Cove, the need to stay disguised and to keep lying about who she really was so she could keep getting information - and the surprising flash of attraction when she met Cullen O'Brien.

It had only been a month since she walked away from Brad. Shouldn't she still be all tied up in the past? Besides, something felt familiar about O'Brien. Fingers trailed through the water before she sat up and blinked. "Shit. O'Brien. I bet he's related to James! Gods, Emlen, you're an idiot."

She climbed out of the tub and grabbed her robe before Emlen went to look for her messenger bag. She eventually found it propped against the entry table. Moments later, she tapped a name on her laptop screen. "Knew it. Cullen O'Brien, thirty-two, son of James. Contractor, self-employed. Graduate of Northeastern University, Criminal Justice. Massachusetts State Police, eight years on the force. Huh." Her voice trailed off as she skimmed the rest of her notes.

"Nothing on if he quit or was fired. Going to have to dig into that one. One brother, Connor, age thirty, also a cop." Closing the laptop, she dropped it on her bed and headed back into the bathroom.

Contacts removed, Emlen stared at her reflection as she rubbed lotion on her face. The dull brown hair dye made her skin seem more pallid than it appeared with her natural auburn hue, but the bright violet of her eyes shone with excitement as she mentally went over the notes. After so many years, she was finally actively doing something—anything—to see if she could find more information on her past. Her deception had worked so far, and she was going to try to keep it going as long as she was able. People spoke more freely when they didn't realize that the person asking the questions had an intimate connection to the story.

Em shut off the light as she stepped into the hallway and froze. Did she see a shadow move? Was there a sound she couldn't identify? Something had her gripping the door frame and shivering in place as the scent of vanilla musk once again wrapped around her. Eyes drifting closed, she could almost feel the comfort of a hug as she let out a slow breath and relaxed. A perfume? Maybe the last tenants had spilled some? A faint shrug and she moved into the bedroom to grab a tank top and sleep shorts before she climbed into bed with her notes and laptop. It would only take her moments to transcribe the conversation with the ladies earlier in the day, adding her own impressions.

The warm breeze through the windows brought the scent of ocean salt and a hint of sea roses. Closing the laptop twenty minutes later, Emlen set everything aside and slid down under the comforter. It would take a few moments to shut her brain down enough to sleep, or so she thought as she turned out the light.

———◦———

He could follow her path through the house as the lights went out, one by one. Cullen stood on his deck and sipped the beer. He watched the lights go out in the kitchen. Then the ones in the bedroom and bath go on. He thought about the pretty girl who was now the girl next door, literally. It wasn't like Cullen didn't have his share of women friends. When he wanted the company, there were those who would be more than happy to climb into his bed. But that wasn't Cullen's style.

He'd played the 'casual sex' game his first couple of years in college – until he'd met Maggie Murphy and decided that he was going to marry her. Maggie, of course, had other ideas, and ended up marrying some doctor's son from Wellesley and had her first kid about two months after graduation.

The beer was warm and going flat by the time Cullen saw the bathroom light go out, then the bedroom one. "Goodnight, Emmy Baldwin. Sweet dreams." He poured the last of the beer over the railing and dropped the bottle into the recycling bin before going back inside.

His house was yet another of the summer cottages that had been slowly turned into a year-round place. Last year, he had taken most of his savings to replace the kitchen and bath. The wide-plank pine glowed with a honeyed warmth beneath the shiny finish, complemented by the black granite counter tops in the kitchen. Doing the work himself meant that the cost had only been in time and materials. He'd taken the time and used quality materials, looking at the project as an investment.

The house had belonged to Camille Brewster's grandmother, Charlotte, until she had died from cancer. Camille had sold it about two months after moving to Muckle Cove. Cullen's father had purchased the house as a rental property and sold it to Cullen three years ago. Years of renters had done more than wear-and-tear damage on the place. A little paint and cleaning just weren't going to cut it. So, he gutted the place, keeping only the crown moldings and fireplace mantel and went to work. Whitewashed beadboard trim and chair railings shone in the great room and the kitchen had walls painted the colors of the sea, sand and sky. Blue in the bath, sea-glass green in the main room and a creamy sand in the kitchen with the tile backsplash done in shades of green and blue tied all of the rooms together.

The upstairs boasted a wet room master bath with multiple shower heads and smoky tiles to complement the carved seashell bowl he'd found and turned into the sink basin. Skylights and French doors out to a small balcony let in tons of light and air, making the space a true refuge.

He'd found a few good pieces of furniture, but he was being particular about what he put in his house. Just last week he'd picked up a Victorian style hall-tree with beveled mirrors and glass-knob coat hooks that, after a few hours of cleaning and polishing, was now residing beside the front door. Cullen liked pieces that had both history and functionality. An antique steamer trunk stored throw blankets and board games and doubled as a coffee table. The wooden hutch in the kitchen not only stored dishes, but held staples like potatoes, onions and flour in the various bins in the base.

As he walked through the house, Cullen turned off the lights and headed up the stairs. He paused at the low cabinet tucked against one wall to pour two fingers of Lagavulin 16, then lifted the glass to breathe in the scent of the whiskey. Once on the balcony, he unwrapped a Hoyo de Monterey Epicure, snipped the end and pocketed the cutters before he dipped the mouth end in the whiskey. A flare of light as he struck the match to touch flame to his cigar. The fragrant smoke swirled around his head as he leaned back into the deck chair and put his feet up on the railing. The stars glimmered overhead, and the constant susurrus of the waves provided a calming backdrop to his thoughts.

The whiskey gone and the cigar half done, Cullen had contemplated staying right where he was for the night when a scream ripped through the quiet and brought him to his feet. It took him a moment to figure out where it had come from, when a second scream had him racing through the house. He grabbed his gun from the shelf by the door and tucked it at his back before he sped across the space between the cottages to Emlen's door.

When he reached the cottage, he pounded on the door and shouted Emmy's name. She opened the door, one hand to hold her robe closed, looking dazed. Cullen grabbed her shoulders as he looked her over as if she were the sole survivor of a catastrophe. "Are you all right, Emmy? Are you hurt?" Cullen's gaze took in the lavender robe that made her eyes seem to glow in a rich amethyst color. Confusion flooded him as he certainly didn't remember her eyes being this color when he saw her earlier.

"I'm fine - what's going on?" Emlen asked, one hand holding the robe tight, the other used to push back sleep-tousled hair. "You do realize it's like two in the morning, right?"

Cullen took a breath and released her, looking past her into the dimly lit house before focusing on her once more. "I heard screams. I thought you were in trouble."

Emlen ducked her head. "Sorry about that. It was probably me having a nightmare."

Tugging his shirt down in back, Cullen made sure his gun was covered up before looking around once more and then back at her. "You sure? Want me to check things out really quick before I go?"

Emlen shook her head before stepping back further. "No, I'm sure it was just a nightmare. I'm so sorry. I'll be sure to shut my windows from now on." Cheeks flushed and her eyes stayed lowered as she reached for the door to pull it towards her.

"No, you don't have to do that. It's too warm to close everything up and who wants to have the air conditioning going all the time?" Cullen tried for a smile, but the adrenaline rush was only now starting to ease off.

"Thanks for checking on me. I'll...uh...good night." Emlen murmured, still not looking up as she shut the door, the snick of the lock settling as Cullen stepped back. His pace back across the stretch between their homes was much slower as he paused now and then to glance back at the now-dark cottage - particularly when he heard the faint 'thump' of a window being shut.

Emlen rested her forehead against the door and quietly groaned. From her first nights at her aunt and uncle's place, to her first nights away at boarding school, the nightmares had always been an issue. Once back in her bedroom, she shut the window firmly and crawled back into bed, thoughts going back to that first night at Emerson. She had warned the R.A. that she needed a private room. That her dreams were disturbing to others. Little did they know that it wasn't her dreams that were disturbing as much as the presence that seemed to come to visit in the dark hours.

"I am NOT sleeping in that room with that weirdo again!" Kate grabbed at her bathrobe ties, hands shaking so that she could barely wrap them around her waist. "She talks in her sleep...and I swear I heard some woman talking back to her."

The R.A. tried to calm Kate down, but she was having none of it.

"I want a roommate that doesn't talk to her dead mother in her sleep. Is that so hard to understand?" Kate yelled.

"No, it's not hard to understand. But if you don't stop shouting, you're going to wake the whole floor." Sue, the resident assistant for Grays Hall, ran a hand through her hair and wondered if the benefits of this job were worth the hassle.

"Joanie is visiting her brother this weekend. Go sleep in her bed for now and I'll do the re-arranging tomorrow, a'ight?" Sue pointed the girl at the other room, walked into Emlen and Kate's room to sit on Kate's bed and look at the other girl.

Emlen sat, knees drawn up, hugging them tightly as she gave a soft sniffle. "I didn't mean to scare her. I was sound asleep, and then she was beating on me with her pillow, telling me to shut up," Emlen whispered, voice thick with tears. "I told them I needed a single room because of my dreams. They didn't want to listen."

Sue sighed and shook her head. "Well, it's a moot point now. Wash your face and I'll make us some tea and then you can maybe go back to sleep? Kate's going to sleep down the hall and we'll get things all moved around tomorrow."

Thick mugs emblazoned with the burgundy emblem of prestige warmed their hands as the tea worked its magic to soothe. "So, what was the dream about?" Susan asked.

Emlen shrugged and sipped the tea, still huddled on her bed, knees drawn up, the mug balanced there with both hands. "It's one I have a lot. I dream my mother's here, talking to me. Telling me things. Begging me to find out who killed her. Then she..." her voice faltered, and Emlen's head bowed as she shook it in denial.

"Your mother was killed?" Susan whispered, the horror in her voice.

"When I was three. We lived on the Cape then." Emlen murmured, sipping the tea once more to forestall any further explanation. Or so she hoped.

"Geez, I'm sorry, Emlen. No wonder you have bad dreams!" Sue was properly horrified and contrite – as they always were – and after a few earnest and hurried sentiments, she made her excuses and left Emlen sitting there with her steaming mug of tea and her thoughts. And the blissfully silent room.

Only in the silence could Emlen feel that comforting touch on her shoulder, or the brush against her cheek - from a hand that could not be seen. Hours of psychiatrists, psychologists, years of medications that did nothing to truly solve the problem had left Emlen determined to find her own solutions for the issues. Usually, meditation, some herbal supplements, and routine kept her from waking up, throat raw from screams and body trembling - but any significant-enough disruption to her schedule could bring them back.

Moving into her childhood home was probably a pretty significant disruption, she thought with a sarcastic snort of wry amusement. Always fragments, the dreams were nothing wholly logical or seemed to be framed in any rationality. More pure emotion than anything else, they left her feeling bereft and adrift, a leaf spinning down a river.

Brad had tried to spend the night a few times, but he always said he 'needed his rest' and would leave shortly after the after-sex cuddling.

Times she spent at his place, they had separate bedrooms and the thick walls kept her disruptions from disturbing anyone else. Thinking about Brad brought her back around to thinking about Cullen and she smiled. Her own knight, rushing to rescue the damsel in distress. How cliché - and yet, oddly comforting. She could never see Brad getting out of bed to check on someone else, never mind racing across the dunes to a neighbor's house. He'd just send a servant or call emergency services. Emlen sighed as she rolled over and closed her eyes, drifting back into sleep. Just before sinking fully under, she felt a hand brush the hair back from her face and the soft press of lips to her brow. A faint smile flickered on her lips as she sank deeper into sleep.

5

Remembrance: Chapter Four

Emlen sat at the breakfast table, a pot of coffee nearby along with the remains of a blueberry muffin from the local bakery. Sunshine streamed through the wide windows, lighting the stacks of papers in the boxes at her feet and glinting off the amber and silver necklace she was absently toying with. Articles and files, photos and scraps of paper were sorted onto chairs, the rest of the table, even a few on the windowsill as she sipped and read. Barnabas curled up on the cushion of the chair next to her in one of the sunbeams.

She didn't have any memories of her own when it came to the O'Briens, other than a faint feeling of having felt safe and loved. Looking at photos of the family and Cullen as a young boy, did nothing to bring her own memories forward. She hadn't even placed the name yesterday when she met him. It took the moment in the bath and the niggling suspicion that she'd missed something important yesterday, to get her to dig in the boxes and realize who Cullen really was.

Sorting the files into chronological order helped her try to order the thoughts and impressions in her own mind. Years of seeing psychologists had taught her to recognize which memories were her own and which were those she'd constructed from others' information. It still terrified her a little to realize that she had so few memories between the ages of three until about age nine. "It was probably all the drugs," she muttered and pulled out the folder on her first few years in school. Two different boarding schools from age five to age eight, before being tutored at her aunt's house for a year with daily psych visits. Fifth grade had her at Emerson Prep, where she managed to stick it out until graduation, thanks to generous donations from her grandparents and uncle. A private suite and half the school funds coming from her family kept the administration from throwing her out.

She'd met Brad at Emerson Prep. Her grandparents had assigned him to her as a date for junior prom. Emlen didn't care a whole lot about things like prom or homecoming. She much preferred hanging out in the library or hiding under the bleachers at the lacrosse field and smoking with her friends. However, junior prom at Emerson was the New England society equivalent of a debutante ball down south, so they buffed and polished and primped, stuffed her into a Dior gown and dusted her with family heirloom jewels before being presented on the arm of Bradley the fifth.

They'd actually had a good time after the first half hour of totally awkward stiffness - about when she'd kicked off her Louboutin's and bribed the live band to play Lady Gaga and got the whole room dancing - even the teachers. He'd brought a flask of eighteen-year-old whiskey and she'd stashed two joints in her pack of cigarettes. They'd ended the night with her sitting on his tux jacket on the roof of the administration building, smoking, drinking and talking until the sun rose and the smell of coffee drifted over from the dining hall.

He'd been fun then, before college graduation and the expectations of his father and the strictures of the family business. Both of their families had agreed that an engagement in their senior year at Harvard was appropriate and a wedding was expected within a year after graduation - but they'd strung it out for over two before she'd finally ended it a month ago.

The heirloom ring was left in the middle of his bed - on top of the photo of Brad kissing Samantha Bishop as she wrapped her legs around his waist. Samantha had been sitting on his desk at Wallingford-Smith and Bishop when Brad's secretary had snapped the photo with her phone and sent it to Emlen.

Aunt Corinne had told Emlen to "let it go", that it was what "all men did" and on and on. Uncle Jon had hugged her and tucked some cash into her purse without Corinne seeing it and whispered that she could do much better than 'Smitty' and waved her off.

It had felt surprisingly liberating to drive away from Beacon Hill with her Range Rover packed up and her GPS set to Muckle Cove.

It was time.

Her mother's murder had been unsolved for twenty years and she needed to at least try. Didn't hurt that she'd already landed two good stories with the New Yorker, one while she was still at Harvard. Freedom to work wherever she wanted - wherever the stories took her - meant she really could stay in the Cove and investigate.

Her first story started out as a stringer piece for the Boston Transcript about sexual harassment in Ivy League schools. It turned into a two-part expose on a sex-for-hire business being run out of several area universities using websites and cell phones to coordinate - and hosted on a well-known tech university's server. That had upset her grandmother to the point where she blamed her grandfather's sudden heart failure and subsequent death on the shame of their granddaughter publishing such 'filth'. It didn't matter to Grandmother that her grandfather had secretly encouraged Emlen by sending her notes and little gifts any time she had something published - whether it be her high school paper or a global magazine.

Emlen had tried for years to be the 'best little girl' possible. It was pointless. Granted, it had been a lot easier to be 'perfect' when she was only home during the holidays, but she was not a society belle and she was pretty sure her mother would never have wanted that for her.

Considering her mom had dragged her to the middle of nowhere in Muckle Cove, it was a pretty good guess.

Her fingers curled around the folder that held the earliest police report on her mother's murder. A wash of fury surged through Emlen as she remembered the first time she'd seen the report, nearly six months ago. She had called in a lot of favors and used some of her reporter's network to get the report.

Opening it, she flipped through the pages until she got to the report from the sheriff, about her. "It wasn't until Camille Brewster's will was read that anyone other than the O'Brien family showed any interest in the welfare of Camille's child, Emlen. Now Camille's sister is quite interested and while I have advocated for Emlen to stay with the O'Brien family, there is nothing I can do. The courts will always go with family over strangers. My heart breaks for the O'Briens. Eileen considers the child a daughter and is not going to handle this well." Emlen closed the file and leaned back. It all made so much sense. Her aunt only wanted her around because of the money.

Well, now all of that money was in Emlen's hands. The full Trust had come to her on her twenty-fifth birthday - about seven months ago. Once she had the money, she'd hired a private investigator and, with a few drinks and dinners, got the files and reports. Brad thought she had become obsessed and unreasonable - that fight had been the last until she got the photo of his 'work activities'. Now, Emlen was here, at the scene of the crime, in the town with the last people to know her mom. If there were any answers, this was the best place to find them.

Emlen sighed and leaned back, closing her eyes. "Mom, I'm going to find who did this. I'm going to get you justice. I swear it." A tear slid down her cheek, then another. She stiffened and sat up quickly at what she would swear was the feel of a hand on her cheek. The whispered words after, had her jumping to her feet, trembling all over.

"I know you will, my jewel."

6

Remembrance: Chapter Five

Every child who has lost a parent imagines the one lost is reaching out to them at some point or another. A song on the radio, a whiff of cologne or perfume, even the sound of the lost one's voice, offering advice or comfort, was not unusual. What was unusual was that Emlen really didn't have many memories to call on. She'd been just shy of four years old when her mother passed. How could she possibly remember the sound of her mother's voice or the scent of her perfume?

Hands shaking, Emlen ran them through her hair and took a few breaths. "Coffee. I need more coffee." She almost spilled it as she refilled her cup and took her seat, sipping the steaming brew. She drank a bit more until her pulse had calmed back down. "Okay, time to set this stuff in order."

Getting to work, she took her sorted piles and put each in a labeled folder before tucking them into a metal file box that was both fireproof and locking. Emlen wasn't taking any chances that the information she'd worked hard to gather would be easily destroyed. Taking the time to start a pot of coffee, Emlen considered her next steps.

Once everything was put away, she pulled her notepad closer and started a list. Now that she had a few more names, she needed to get more information, starting with Cullen O'Brien. A moment of weirdness as she realized the hot guy she had been checking out had almost become her brother. "Now, that would have been a disappointment." She laughed to herself and kept writing.

She wanted to find out about the sheriff, Joel Desantis, who had run the case in the beginning. Other officers that had any contact, any people they had considered suspects and even James O'Brien, Cullen's father went on the list. She wanted to know about Cullen's brother Connor, too - where was he? What did he possibly know? Both Cullen and Conner were old enough that they may well remember bits that might be helpful. She also had to corner her uncle and find out what he knew, if anything, about what had driven her mother to leave New York and come to the Cove.

Every time she'd asked him or her aunt about her mother, they'd changed the subject. It didn't take her long to figure out that Camille was considered the 'black sheep' of the family and a disgrace they didn't care to discuss. After reading the police report comments by Sheriff Desantis, she understood even better why they had left her with the O'Brien family until the will had been probated.

Em locked the box then shoved it into the cabinet in the kitchen island and set the stand mixer in front so it wasn't easy to see at first glance. A quick look around and the only thing left out was her notepad, pen and a few empty file folders. Em pulled her Glock from her bag and slid it into the credenza drawer by the door. Permits and all, it was still not something she was comfortable carrying all the time.

Just then, a knock on the door made her jump. She took a breath, her hand pressed to her chest as she worked to slow her startle reflex. Another slow breath as she passed the table and flipped the notebook closed on the way to the door. Emlen peeked outside and she couldn't hide the smile as she opened the door. "Good morning, Cullen. What brings you to my door?"

Cullen held up a bakery bag and grinned. "Wanted to welcome my new neighbor with some of the best pastries in the Cove."

"Sounds great. Come on in. I even have a fresh pot of coffee nearly done."

Cullen stepped inside "A match made in heaven - coffee and Ma Bressette's apple and strawberry turnovers. I didn't know which you might like, so I got some of both. She also makes peach and cherry, but nine a.m. is too late to get those when the tourists are still in town."

"Well, it's good that you got my two favorites then," she replied as she headed to the cabinet to pull out a clean mug and grabbed the fresh pot of coffee to bring to the table.

"Were you working?" Cullen asked when he saw the notebook, pen, folders and cup on the table. "I'm sorry, I should've called first."

"Just sorting through some files and making notes on my next story," Emlen said, pouring him his coffee. "Sugar? Cream?"

"Naw, black is fine," he replied, settling in the seat opposite her workspace, the bag set on the table between them. "Got a plate and some napkins? These are messy. So much so that my brother calls them more finger-lickin' good than that chicken stuff."

Barnabas came in then and started twining around Cullen's feet, begging for a treat. Reaching down, Cullen scritched the cat and looked up at Emlen.

Laughing, Emlen grabbed a plate and some napkins and set them down on the table before she took her seat and put her things aside. "Your brother? Where is Connor now? Still in the Cove?"

The look of surprise on Cullen's face had her realizing her mistake as she looked up at him and he paused mid sip, setting down his mug and really looking at her. "Your eyes..."

"Oh. Shit." Emlen whispered and put her hands over her face.

"Oh shit...what?" he asked, tone chilling.

"I forgot my contacts."

"So, it would seem. How about you tell me what's really going on here?" Cullen demanded, both hands now on the edge of the table as he leaned a little closer.

"I didn't mean for you to find out like this. I was going to tell you later today, but you surprised me. See...we knew each other a long time ago."

Slowly, Emlen lifted her gaze to meet his and sighed. "But I need you to keep this quiet, all right? It's important."

Cullen stared into her brilliant violet eyes and his own widened. "Emlen Brewster." His smile slowly grew. "Goddamn Emlen Brewster! Oh, my folks are gonna be so glad to hear you're alive and doing okay." He reached for her hand and then paused. "Wait...keep it quiet? Why? Don't you realize how many people in this town would be thrilled to know you're back?"

"Cullen, you can't! I need to stay under the radar for now. I'm here, investigating my mother's murder." Emlen shot to her feet and started to pace. "Look, I know your family was good to me after it all happened, even though I don't remember it, I appreciate it. But I've been using an alias and disguise so I could get information without people figuring out it's me that's asking. Please..." she turned, hands clasped together as she pleaded with him. "...please keep my secret. Just for a while longer, okay?"

"Hey, easy. I'll keep it for now." Cullen offered his agreement and sighed. "But this is crazy, you know that, right? It's not safe. They never caught the guy that did it." Leaning back in the chair, he looked at her and shook his head. "I used to be a cop. I did some of my own investigating on the case, back when I was on the force. A couple of months after I started digging, something went down - something really bad - and I ended up quitting police work. Nothing I found was news or gave us any new leads. I don't see—"

Emlen cut him off. "I'm one of the best investigative reporters out there right now. If there is something to find, I'll find it." She sat again and reached for her cup, fingers tightening around the mug. "I'm not restrained by the same limitations a cop would be."

"You still need to be careful," Cullen grumbled as he pulled pastries out of the bag and stacked them on the plate. He was quiet while they each took one and started to eat. He put his down on the napkin and looked up at her. "You're not doing this alone. I'm in."

"Wait, what? No, you're not in this. She was my mother. This is my investigation."

"And if you want me to keep your secret, you'll let me help."

"That's blackmail!"

"Yeah, it is. But I don't need to lose any more sleep, worrying about you, all right? Just be gracious and accept my help. I won't get in your way, but hey, I still have cop skills that may come in handy."

She thought about it for a moment, then sighed. "Yeah, I guess. But this is my investigation. No high-handed control grabs. Got it?"

"Got it," Cullen said, then grinned. "Wow, I can't believe I'm sitting here with Emlen Brewster. Mom got copies of your New Yorker stories and put them in her scrapbook. She followed your life as best she could, but it was like you disappeared the day they took you away." His smile faded, and he looked down into his cup. "Mom cried for weeks." Cullen shook his head slightly, looking back up at her. "And you don't remember anything from that time?"

"No, not really. I get flashes of things - a woman rocking me in a chair and singing to me, a tall man letting me ride on his shoulders, but no real clear memories. My therapist says it was blocked by the shock and trauma." Em's fingers picked at the flaky pastry bits on her plate. "I don't even have any memories of this place from that time, other than a couple of times my uncle brought me back to town to sign paperwork when I was older."

"You know my Dad was a suspect for a while because he was the one that found you and your Mom's body, right?" Cullen watched her face as he spoke.

"Yeah, I read that in the reports. They brought him in for questioning, but his alibi was solid and he had no motive. That, and if he'd really done it, I doubt they would've left me with your family for months."

"True, but it still ruined his life for a while. We even moved out of the cove for a few years to let things die down. His business was failing because people didn't want to hire the guy that 'maybe' killed a young mother. They came back so Connor and I could finish high school where my dad and his father and his father's father had gone to school, but it was tough. I bought the house from Dad, and he and Mom retired to Florida. Connor lives just outside of Boston - he's a state cop now."

"So, you and Connor both became cops?"

"Because of what happened, yeah. Both to you and your mom, and to my folks during the investigation. It bugged us that no one had been able to solve the case, so we decided we were going to be cops when we got older so we could solve it and show everyone, once and for all, it was never my Dad."

"I get that," Emlen murmured, refilling their mugs and leaning back, gaze shifting from Cullen's face to the view outside the window. Sunshine sparkled on the waves where a small sailboat skidded past, leaving a wake. "I'm sorry about what happened to your family."

Cullen blinked at her. "My family? Jeezus, Emlen, your family was taken from you. Yeah, my family had shit to deal with, but we got through it all together. I remember when your aunt came to take you away. You refused to let go of my Mom; she had to untangle your arms and hold you out away from her. Then your aunt grabbed you and slapped you. I thought my mother was going to beat your aunt right there and then. She turned away and staggered back to the house, her face white, her fingers clenched in fists so tight, her nails cut her palms. She wanted to keep you - considered you hers after all the time that had passed. Guess it was the money or something. They'd never talk about it, but I found Desantis' report and read what he said."

"It was. I've seen that report, only just recently, and it explained a lot. I spent a lot of time at boarding schools," Emlen said. "They can't touch the money now, though. At least my uncle was smart enough to make good investments for me and keep my aunt's hands off of the majority of it."

"I'm sorry." He reached for her hand, taking it in his own. His thumb rubbed over her knuckles and he gave her a wry smile. "I'm really glad you were going to tell me, Emlen. I'm just going to find it tough to not tell my family you're here and you're okay. Don't make me wait too long to let them know, all right?"

"I'm glad I told you too. I realized I probably should when you were so kind yesterday, but I was afraid you'd not be so understanding about why I was hiding who I am." His touch sent a flare of warmth from her fingers to her belly and she let out a shaky laugh. "And as weird as it sounds, I'm glad we didn't end up siblings."

He laughed too and lifted her hand, kissing her fingers. "Oh, yeah, that would've made this really weird - because I find myself attracted to you, Miss Brewster." Releasing her hand, he nodded to the window. "Want to get out of here for a bit? Let's go for a walk on the beach and enjoy the day before it gets too warm, shall we?"

"Sounds like a plan. Let me get my shoes and lock up." Picking up their mugs, she put them in the sink and grabbed her shoes, keys and phone and met him by the kitchen door. "Thanks again for this, Cullen."

"For what?"

"For understanding and being so welcoming. I'd forgotten what it was like to be around genuinely nice people."

Cullen held the door for her and made sure it was locked behind them before taking her hand and heading down the weathered steps to the beach. "It makes me sad and angry to realize how little basic kindness you've experienced. I'll have to see what I can do to change that for you."

Em pretended to not have heard him as they climbed over the rocks to the beach below.

7

Remembrance: Chapter Six

The walk on the beach had turned into dinner at Cullen's place with a lot of laughter and stories shared from their childhoods. He'd kissed her goodnight when he left her at her door and Emlen still got a little grin on her lips when she thought of it. He was taking it slow and she was grateful. Even thought she had been done with Brad for a while, it was good to get to know Cullen as a friend first, considering everything else she had on her plate.

A few articles on local events had made it to her usual sources and after almost two weeks in the Cove, Emlen felt settled and comfortable. And nervous. Today, Emlen and Cullen were going to sit down with Joel Desantis, the man who had been sheriff in the Cove when the murder happened. In his late sixties now, Desantis lived in a small house out on the point - the tip of the cove's curl of rocks before the open sea.

Checking her messenger bag once again, Emlen made sure she had notepad, pens, micro recorder, phone, keys and copies of a few pages of the police report in the event she had to help his memory. Cullen said he was still sharp, but she'd rather have too much information than need it and not have the notes.

She couldn't wait in the house any longer, so Emlen grabbed her keys and locked the door behind her, taking a seat in the glider on the side porch. The glitter of the water caught her attention and she sighed, setting the seat rocking as she tracked a sailboat across the cove towards the pier on the south end.

Cullen was nice - really nice - and she felt a little guilty, using him like this. Oh, she could have probably managed to get the interview with Desantis without him, but it was a lot easier to use Cullen's connections. Whatever it took to get the answers she wanted - no, needed - then she'd do it. She owed it to her mother to find out what happened and get her justice. It was what had driven her, motivated her, even when everyone around her told her she should let it go, leave it to the professionals, and so on. It was why she'd pushed herself to be the best investigative reporter she could become. Her aunt had wanted her to go for a business degree or political science or something that would bring more prestige to the family name - but that wasn't Emlen's path, no more than it had been her mother's path.

She could still hear her aunt's strident tone. "You'll attend Wellesley and major in business or political science." Corinne stood there, hands on hips, glare firmly in place.

"Not interested." Emlen replied, smirking beneath the fall of her hair as she finished packing her bag.

"I don't care if you're 'interested'," Corinne sneered. "You'll do as you're told."

"Right, because that's worked so well for me in the past. No, Auntie. I'm going to Harvard and majoring in Journalism. I've already enrolled, and I'll be starting in the fall." Shouldering her bag, she tugged the handle of her suitcase and started it rolling as she walked towards the door.

"I see. Well, I hope you don't expect us to pay for your decision," Corinne said, ice in her tone.

"Of course not. Why would you? Doesn't matter. I got a scholarship and I have a job, so I can manage."

"And where are you going right now?" Her aunt only just now seemed to notice that Emlen was packed more than a weekend would require.

"Moving in with my roommates. We got an off-campus place that four of us are sharing. I'm eighteen now, so you're not responsible for me any longer. I'm sure that will be a relief."

"Your uncle and I did not approve of this. I forbid it." Corinne folded her arms under her breasts and glared at Emlen.

"Go ahead and forbid it all you want, Auntie. Not your call anymore. Thanks for nothing," Emlen replied and headed out the door, letting the suitcase thump down the stairs behind her just to irritate her ice bitch aunt, her grin growing as she stepped outside and took a breath of air. Freedom was a heady thing.

The sound of Cullen's truck pulling up on the gravel tugged Emlen from her memories. She got to her feet, still grinning at the memory, a hint of challenge in her step as she headed towards the passenger's door.

"Nice to see you, Cullen. Appreciate your help with this," she said as she slid into the truck and dropped her bag at her feet.

"Happy to help," Cullen said, glancing over at her as she snapped her seatbelt. "You look like someone pissed in your cereal this morning. What's up?"

"Nothing, really. Just remembering a time when I kicked ass." Emlen said as she gave him a sidelong look. "Seriously, I'm good. Let's go see if the old sheriff has any new leads for us, shall we?"

"When I called, he said he'd have his box of files out for us to go over, too. Maybe there's something in there that we've not seen before. Honestly, he's going to be our best option."

"I just hope he's still sharp. I can't tell you how many retired people I've interviewed that I ended up spending weeks researching their intel to find out they didn't have a clue as to what they were remembering."

Cullen slowed the truck and stared at her for a moment before his gaze went back to the road. "Uncle Joel is as sharp as they come. His reaction time slowed down a bit and he didn't want to be too slow on the trigger and cost someone their life - or cost him his own - just because age had settled in." His tone icy, he gripped the steering wheel, glaring at the road.

"Uncle Joel?" Emlen smirked and shook her head. "Relax, Cullen. I wasn't actually insulting the guy. I've never met him, remember? Just stating how things usually play out."

"Pretty negative way to look at things, don'tcha think? And you have met him before, you just don't remember."

"Why is it negative when it's based on fact?"

"Have you ever heard of the "it's all in the mindset" approach? If you go into it, expecting negative results, you'll get negative results - but if you go into it expecting positive, you get positive?" Cullen asked, turning on to the gravel road that led towards Desantis' cottage.

"Yeah, isn't there a fortune cookie quote about that?" she snarked back and turned to look out the window. "I'm more along the lines of Bruce Lee, when he said, "I'm not in this world to live up to your expectations and you're not here to live up to mine." And I'm probably paraphrasing it, but that's pretty close."

Stopping the truck, Cullen pulled the key as he gave her a brief look before starting to get out of the car. "Good thing I don't have any expectations then."

"That makes one of us," Emlen said as she shouldered her bag and slammed the truck door shut. Her tone calmly conversational, she added "You fuck this up for me and it'll be the last thing we ever do together." She had been enjoying his company, but the idea of sharing the investigation at all made her want to choke. The rollercoaster of her own emotions made her dizzy.

"Hey there!" Joel called out from the side deck of the house, waving at them as they walked up towards him. "Perfect day for enjoying the view, eh?"

"Thanks for taking the time to meet with me." Emlen replied, stepping up to the deck and offering a hand to shake. "I really appreciate it."

"Anything for the O'Brien boys, Joel replied, shaking her hand. "And I am really glad to see you're doing so well, Emlen Brewster. Don't worry, I'll keep your secret. Cullen explained it all to me and I understand."

Cullen walked up and moved to give Joel a brief hug and a back slap. "Looking good, Uncle Joel. How's the fishing been?"

The two men laughed as they led the way into the house, Emlen trailing behind and taking a moment to enjoy the view of the mouth of the cove and the open sea beyond. "Bet this is an impressive view in a storm," she said as she paused before stepping inside.

"It really is. Nothing better than a hot cup of coffee, a fire in the woodstove and the power of nature dancing outside my window," Joel answered, gesturing to seats around a table set before one of the many wide windows. A carafe of coffee sat on the table with a cluster of mugs, spoons stuck into another mug and a plate of cookies. A box resting on a chair drew Emlen's interest. Seeing her stare, Joel nodded. "Yeah, that's one box of my notes on this case. The other two are on the floor by the door, but this one has more of what I think you want to talk about."

The three of them sat, and Joel poured them coffee before he folded his hands around the mug and looked up at Emlen. Silent for a moment, he searched her face, then gave her a small smile. "I still see you in my mind, that little bit of a thing, wrapped up in a towel, sitting on Jaime's truck seat, bottle of water clutched in your hands." He shook his head and took a sip of the coffee. "What your family did still pisses me off, but I'm glad to see you're successful and healthy and all that. I just wish you hadn't come back to town."

"Wait, what? What are you saying that for, Uncle Joel?" Cullen blurted. "You trying to scare her off or something?"

Emlen leaned back and sipped her own coffee as she watched the two, letting the dynamics play out in front of her as she listened and learned. A feeling twinged at the back of her mind and she focused on Joel for a few moments before letting out a soft breath.

"Easy, Cull. I just mean, it's not safe for her, being back here. Whoever killed her mom, searched the house for her, too." Joel reached into the box, pulling out a worn folder and laying it on the table. One hand rested on top of it as he spoke. "Cull told me that you'd already seen the official report, so I won't insult you by warning you about what's in here - but I am going to ask for my own peace of mind - are you sure you want to see this?"

Emlen reached out, resting one hand on top of Joel's on the folder. "I appreciate your consideration, sir. I truly do - but I need to see it all." A faint smile curled her lips and she shifted her hand to grasp the folder to tug it a little closer.

"Okay, well, take a look at the top few photos," Joel replied, voice a little rough.

Opening the folder, the photos were eight by tens of the crime scene, but photos neither Emlen nor Cullen had yet seen. They showed a man's boot prints, tracking blood throughout the house, leaving marks on carpets and floors. It clearly showed the path of someone who had searched every closet and room.

"I still don't know how he didn't find you." Joel spoke quietly. "Do you remember where you were hiding?"

"In the window seat," Emlen replied, then blinked and looked up at him, only now having just remembered it. Shuffling through the photos, she found one that showed the grate-covered window seat in the living room. "I was in there. When Mama heard someone in the house, she pulled out a blanket, put me in there and then closed it up and put the cushion and blanket back on top. She told me to not make a sound until she came to get me out."

"That's in the room she was found in, correct?" Joel asked, his voice soft.

"Yeah. I must've seen the whole thing, but I don't remember. I didn't even remember hiding in there until you asked just now." Emlen slid the photos over each other, looking at the rest in the folder. Closing her eyes, she tried to see if any other memories would surface, but nothing did. "I'm sorry, I can't seem to remember anything else right now."

"Did you ever try hypnosis or anything like that?" Cullen asked, sipping his coffee.

"I think one of the many psychiatrists I saw as a kid might have tried it, but no real results."

"It's pretty clear, though, that you do have some repressed memories," Joel said. "Maybe it's something to consider trying again. Not that I put a lot of stock in hypnosis, and not like any recovered memories from something like that would be admissible in court, but maybe it'd help you?"

"Then again, her memories may be buried to protect her from what she saw," Cullen replied.

"True, that's possible as well." Joel looked over at Emlen. "Just something to think about, I guess, eh?"

"Yeah, something to think about. So, what else do you have in there?" Emlen slid the photos back into the folder and set it aside.

Two hours later, Emlen had pages of notes and they'd only gone through one of the two boxes set near the table. Joel started another pot of coffee and made some sandwiches. Cullen stacked files back into the box and cleared the table for food.

As she flipped through her notes, Emlen added comments now and again before asking, "Joel, I know we've seen the photos and such, but I know that 'cop instinct' is a real thing. I would like to know what your thoughts were that day and what they are now, all these years later."

Joel brought out the sandwiches and put the plates in front of each of them before he grabbed a bag of chips and dumped a few on his own plate. As he sat back down, he grabbed a chip and washed it down with a sip of coffee. "Let me speak plain here. I think whoever killed your mother was supposed to kill you and if they figure out that you're back in Muckle Cove, they will try again."

"Then we have to make sure Em stays secret," Cullen replied. "No one outside of the three of us should know she's back in town."

Emlen raised her hand in a 'stop' motion, glaring at Cullen. "Didn't we already talk about this?" Her gaze shifted to take in both men. "Look, most of my life, other people decided what I would do and where I would go and how I would get there. No one has done that for me since I was eighteen years old and no one is about to start that now. Are we clear yet?"

"And you came here for my information and my advice." Joel answered calmly. "So, here's my advice. Keep your identity hidden and be careful who you question, what questions you ask. You survived once. There's no guarantee you'll survive a second attempt."

"How certain are you that there will be a second attempt?" Cullen asked.

"Try third or fourth attempt," Joel said. "There was another attempt while Emlen was living with your parents, Cullen. We think there was one when she was about nine or ten. That last one was handled by the Brewster's security team."

Emlen sucked in a breath, staring at Joel, eyes wide. "I had a class trip when I was nine. Just before they pulled me out of school. One of my bodyguards disappeared on the trip and when we got back to school, I was called to the office and taken home. Aunt Corinne said it was because I was a troublemaker." The residual fear was soon overtaken by anger. "I thought it was all my fault I was stuck with a home tutor for a year. That fucking bitch said that Andrews was fired because I was bad!"

"Andrews. Christopher Andrews was found shot to death in an alley behind the Smithsonian a day after your class trip. I got a report on it because I had tags on all of your bodyguards and relatives," Joel told her.

He got up and went to one of the boxes by the door and opened it, flipping through folders until he pulled one free and walked back over to place it in front of her. "He was shot by another one of your guards when he tried to take you out." News articles and photos of the crime scene spilled across the table as Emlen flipped it open and skimmed the information.

"He used to bring me cherry Cokes when my aunt wouldn't let me have soda." Emlen murmured softly as she put the papers back into the folder and closed it. "Any information on who hired him?" Her hands trembled a little as she smoothed them over the folder, then pushed it closer to Joel, reaching for her coffee to take a couple of swallows.

"No, but it is pretty clear that it's someone with resources. It looks like after you went to Emerson, word got out that you didn't have any memories and they backed off. Which is why if word gets out that you're researching this now, they'll come after you again."

Cullen looked from Joel to Emlen as they talk and he nodded, "Yeah, that makes a lot of sense, Uncle Joel." Then he turned to Emlen. "Do you have any idea who your father is?"

A shake of her head and Emlen sighed. "No. Aunt Corinne probably has some suspicion, but she would never tell me. I'm pretty sure grandmother knows but she would cut out her own tongue before she'd ever say. All I know is that he has the same color eyes I have, because my grandmother would tell me to stop looking at her with my father's eyes when she was really angry with me over something."

"And you have unusual eyes, but that still won't narrow down the field." Joel offered, lifting his mug in a faint salute.

"She was wearing contacts when I first saw her back in town." Cullen added, chuckling.

"And I dye my hair. It's normally a lot more red. Subtle change, but it works." Emlen added as she toyed with her necklace.

"Subtle changes are usually the most effective. Make it too dramatic a change and people's brains register that something is 'off'. It makes them look twice or remember you when you're trying to be easily forgotten," Joel replied. He paused, then smiled down at the pendant caught in her fingers. "I see you still have your mother's necklace."

"Of course. It's one of the few things I have of hers. I always keep it close. I promised I would." A frown furrowed Emlen's brow for a moment and then she sighed. "At least, I promised someone. I think it was her. It's not a clear memory, but I know I have to have it with me always. It keeps me safe."

"Talismans are powerful things," Joel assured her. "I remember when your mother sent it to be blessed at the Vatican before she gave it to you."

"The Pope blessed this? Wow." Em lifted the amber and silver piece and it sparkled in the sunlight. "That's pretty impressive. Not that I follow any particular faith, but still..."

A wry grin curled Joel's lips. "Faith doesn't need a religion to exist. Protection comes from many things. Just glad to see you still honor her wishes."

Cullen watched the interplay, a slight frown creased his brow. He raised an eyebrow at Joel who pursed his lips and gave the tiniest of head shakes.

"Joel, are you okay with me having your number and calling with any other questions? I'd like to take this stuff home and spend some time going over it and then talk to you again." Emlen asked as she got to her feet and stuffed her notes and gear into her bag.

"Of course, give me your phone and I'll add it," he replied, doing just that as she handed her phone over while Cullen gathered some of the boxes and headed out to the car.

Emlen turned back to Joel as he handed the phone back. "I really appreciate everything you've done...and everything you did back then. I'm glad you understand how important this is to me, and how valuable it is for me to have you on my side."

"Oh, Emlen, you don't have to thank me. Every cop has that one case that haunts them, and this one is mine. If I can help you find some answers, it would go a long way towards bringing me some peace, too."

Emlen gave him a hug as Cullen stepped back in to grab the last of the boxes and smiled as he watched them. "Take care of yourself, Joel." Emlen murmured and turned toward the door.

She paused, that little twinge in the back of her mind prodding her as she turned to him and murmured, "Joel, is your health good? Maybe get a checkup or something?"

"Now why would you say that?" Joel asked, a brow arching as he looked at her.

"Just a feeling. You're a treasure and we don't want to lose you," Emlen replied and offered a weak smile as she turned to the door.

"See you Sunday, Uncle Joel," Cullen called out and stepped outside, following Emlen to the car.

"Sunday? What are you doing on Sunday?" Emlen asked as she slid into the passenger's seat.

"Uncle Joel and I go fishing every Sunday. He used to go with my dad, but Dad's in Florida now, so I stepped up and started going with him. Joel's family, in all the ways that matter."

"Blues are running now, right?" Emlen asked. "I'd like to invite myself to go along with you if that's okay?"

Driving down the road, Cullen glanced over and smiled. "Are you really this perfect? Smart, beautiful -and- you like to fish? Next you'll tell me you're a Red Sox fan and I'll have to marry you."

They both laughed as he headed back towards her cottage.

8

Remembrance: Chapter Seven

Joel watched the truck pull away and let his shoulders sag. The weight of his knowledge was almost more than he could take after seeing her again. He headed back inside, gathered a few things and sat down at his table once more. Now that the girl was back, he had arrangements to take care of, to make sure the next in line would be ready when they came for him.

"I failed your mother, Emlen, but I won't fail you. I'll see that your Garda is one worthy of the task." Joel whispered to himself as he sealed the letter with red wax and the imprint of his signet ring. The ring and the letter went into a small box and that was tucked into one of the many hidden niches in his house. Sitting and looking out at the water, he watched the sun start to set before he pulled out his phone and made the call.

"Garda DeSantis, it's been a long time." the voice answered.

"Aye, it has. The girl is back, and she still wears the druid egg," Joel replied.

"Splendid. As long as she stays subdued, there is no need for action."

"She's investigating her mother's murder. I've chosen my successor in the event that her being back here brings events into play once more."

"Understood. The O'Brien boy, correct?"

"Yes, Your Eminence. Cullen. He's already invested, so it won't take much to get him to commit."

"Your judgement has never been in question, Joel. Camille's death is not on you. You were to protect the child, not the mother, and you did.

Keep us informed as to the progress. Beannachtaí ar do shon."

"Blessings unto you as well, Your Eminence. Good night." Joel's hand shook a little as he set the phone down and rubbed his face. He was getting too old for this. The games and power plays got more difficult as time wore on. He just hoped he had the time he needed to get things in place now that she was back.

Her question about his health had every hair standing up on the back of his neck. He knew he was healthy for a man of his age. It could only be her gift, giving him a warning. Joel pushed to his feet and headed deeper into his home. The list of what needed to be done was long, and he was running out of time.

9

Remembrance: Chapter Eight

Four days later, Emlen was dressed in jeans, boots, t-shirt and sweatshirt, a cooler in hand and a bag over her shoulder, standing outside and waiting for Cullen. The sun just started to tint the dark edges of the horizon, the chill of the ocean breeze making her grateful for the sweatshirt. She found herself excited about this trip - it had been a few years since she'd gone fishing. The last time was with Brad and his friends, who had been more interested in partying on the boat than actually fishing.

Cullen pulled up and she put the cooler in the back of the truck, tucking the bag between her feet as she settled into the cab.

"Excited?" Cullen asked.

"Yeah, actually I am," Em replied, grinning. "I packed a picnic lunch for the three of us."

"Well, it'll just be the two of us today," Cullen replied. "Joel had tickets to see the Sox play so he headed into Boston. It'll be just us."

"Well, more sandwiches and beer for us then!"

"I hope it's good beer and none of that watered-down cheap crap, Cullen threatened, laughing low. "I'm Irish, I won't drink bad beer."

"Don't worry, O'Brien. I got a couple of different craft beers and I didn't buy canned Guinness because I remember you making faces at the commercial the other day."

"Observant. Is that part of your investigative reporting training?"

"Naw, just a skill I learned. I picked up a lot of cop-type skills over the years. See, when you have bodyguards around as a kid, you emulate the adults around you. When I was a teenager, I got them to take me to the firing range and teach me how to shoot. I got hand-to-hand training and everything. It's been useful on a few stories I was working on."

Pulling up at the pier, Cullen turned to look at her. "I'm glad to hear it. We can hit the range sometime if you like?"

"Yeah, sounds good. Now, which boat is yours?" Emlen asked, gazing out at the collection of pleasure boats and working craft.

Pointing to a boat about halfway down the pier, he grinned. "That's my baby. A Stingray Cuddy cabin cruiser. Why don't we stop and get the bait at the shop there first?" A shack sat on the right side of the pier, stacked with lobster traps, netting and a wooden barrel full of rods.

"Good plan. Kinda hard to catch fish without bait." Emlen pulled the cooler out of the truck and slid the bag over her shoulder. "You got the rods?" Cullen held up the bag with the gear and reached out a hand to take hers. Fingers entwined, they stepped into the shop.

"Frankie! Hook us up, man!" Cullen called out as he headed over to the rough wood counter just inside the door. "Going out for some blues and whatever else we can catch."

The man behind the counter was easily early fifties and about that many pounds overweight. Bald with a tangled beard that hung down his chest, Frankie waved jovially to Cullen. "Pail or bucket, Cull?"

"Bucket!" Emlen called out. "We're going to catch our weight in fish."

Frankie's gaze went to Emlen and his smile faded a little. "Who's the lady, Cull?"

"This is Emmy Baldwin, my girl. Taking her out on The Colleen today."

Emlen got a little thrill from Cullen's statement and grinned up at him before turning to Frankie. "Nice to meet you, Frankie."

Untangling her fingers from Cullen's, she offered a handshake to Frankie - but Frankie just stared at her, not reaching for her hand.

"You from 'round here?" Frankie asked, eyes narrowing as he examined her face. "Look kinda familiar."

Letting her hand drop, Emlen glanced from Frankie to Cullen and back. "No, from Boston area mostly. Just moved to town recently."

"Got that bucket, Frankie?" Cullen interrupted, stepping in front of Emlen, breaking Frankie's stare. "We want to get out on the water before the sun comes up."

———

Emlen stepped back closer to the door, her own attention now locked firmly on Frankie as he put a plastic bucket of bait on the counter and rang up the sale. She watched through the slats of a shelf, making it difficult for Frankie to see her, and he did keep trying to get a better look at her while handling the bait sale. Finally, she slipped outside and shifted so she could watch through the edge of the window. As Cullen stepped out, she kept her gaze on the window and muttered, "The way he was watching me was creepy." She turned to walk with Cullen as Frankie disappeared towards the back of the shack.

"Yeah, it was a little odd, but then Frankie's always been a little odd.

Joel brought him in a few times for drunk and disorderly, had him sleeping it off in the jail at least three times a month. Then his father died and left him the bait shop and he cleaned himself up enough to keep the business going." Cullen led her to the boat and helped her aboard before handing her the gear bag. "Here, stow this over there by the bench and I'll get the lines."

Tucking the bags and cooler against the bench, Emlen caught the first rope and coiled it up, stepping back as Cullen jumped aboard with the other. He coiled it, tucking it away before heading to the console and starting up the engines.

Dropping into the second seat near the console, Emlen glanced back at the pier as they pulled away and spotted Frankie standing a few feet from the shack, a phone to his ear. A shiver ran through her as she looked away towards the open ocean.

"I swear, it was her." Frankie said into the phone. "She had blue eyes and dark hair, but she looks just like her mother."

"You still need to finish the job," the voice replied. "Take care of it. Once and for all."

"Yes, sir, I will."

"And don't fuck it up this time, or you'll be lying right next to your Daddy." *click*

Frankie looked at the phone and then out to the boat heading to the open water. He had plans to make and things to do.

10

Remembrance: Chapter Nine

A fist slammed down on the mahogany desk, the heavy signet ring leaving a gouge in the wood. "I thought you said she didn't have any memories! What the hell is she doing back in that godforsaken shit hole if she doesn't remember?" Judge Jackson glared at his guest.

A pampered hand slid over a silk-clad leg as the woman sitting across from him smoothed her pants, the glint of gold and diamonds sparkling in the lamplight. "She doesn't remember, but she still owns the house in the Cove. It's probably just sentimentality. Remember, she's recovering from a broken engagement."

"Still trying to keep your granddaughter alive, old woman?"

"Of course. The sheer amount of money I've spent on that girl, I'd like to see some return on my investment." Emilia Brewster swirled the drink in her hand.

A low chuckle and the man lifted the Baccarat crystal tumbler, taking a sip of his Eagle Rare bourbon. "Always about the money with you, isn't it?"

"Well, you paid me enough to stay silent regarding Camille's elimination. I've made sure that her daughter wouldn't remember, and anything she did would be questioned. Who is going to believe the tangled memories of a girl who spent years under psychiatric care? No one."

"True, but I'm in a precarious position. One story by an intrepid reporter, there will be questions and doubt, and he'll lose his bid. You want to talk about investments? One woman's life is nothing compared to what I've got on the line."

"You'll do whatever you think is best, as always." Rising to her feet, she put her untouched drink down on the desk and collected her purse. "I'd appreciate it if you left her alive a little bit longer. She still hasn't signed her will."

"You've got a week." The door closed behind her, leaving a cloud of Chanel behind as he drained his glass and set it on the desk. "A week, and then she dies. And so do you."

11

Remembrance: Chapter Ten

They'd had a great time fishing and only brought a couple home each, spending the night frying fish over a campfire on the beach and drinking beer that they hadn't got to while on the boat. Sprawled on a blanket by the dying fire, they were enjoying a few kisses when Cullen pulled back and cupped her face. "Stay with me tonight." he asked, voice soft.

"Tempting, but I should probably sleep in my own bed tonight." Emlen tangled her fingers in his hair and tugged him down for another kiss. "As much as I'd like to sample more than your kisses, I've only been out of a long-term relationship for a few weeks. I don't want you to be a rebound. You deserve better than that."

"Beautiful, brilliant and a kind heart, Cullen murmured, kissing again. "All right, lovely. On your schedule and in your time."

"Thank you." Emlen smiled, kissed him again and got to her feet, starting to gather the things. "No, leave it. I'll clean it up. Let me walk you home and then I'll come back."

She dumped sand over the dying fire and Emlen put the bucket down before picking up her bag. "Okay, Romeo." She laughed and held out her hand to him. Fingers entwined, they headed up the beach towards the cottage.

It had been a little more difficult to get into the cottage this time than it had been before, but his skills were still good enough to bypass the locks. Frankie didn't even consider the windows, not at this stage of the game. Oh, yeah, when he was twenty years younger and about sixty pounds lighter, he might have, but not now.

He'd seen the two down on the beach and figured the way they were going at it, he had plenty of time to take a look around. He'd already found the cardboard boxes of files and papers and a stack of notepads that would give the boss a coronary when he told him. He took a few more shots of the documents with his phone and then stuffed it in his pocket.

Taking the folders out of the box, he spilled them out on the floor, making sure all of the folders were emptied and spread around. He tore the pages out of the notepads and scattered them with the rest. Then he took a bottle of bleach and spilled it over all of the pages, the boxes and the laptop on the table. He'd taken several bottles out from under the sink and started spilling them all over everything. Vinegar, carpet cleaner, scrubbing cleanser, each making more of a mess on the pile of pages and photos.

Fumes rose from the pile and Frankie coughed and stepped back. Reaching for the laptop, he grabbed it with both hands and smashed it against the table a few times, damaging the table and destroying the laptop before he dropped it into the mess on the floor. "Good luck researching now, little girl." He chuckled and headed for the door, then ducked behind a bush as they entered the house. Waiting until they were inside, Frankie headed back to his van. He saved his laughter until he got away from the cottage.

He wanted to take her out tonight, but not with the boy there. He wasn't getting paid to kill Cullen, just her - and he hated the boss enough to not give him a freebie.

"Thanks for a great evening," Emlen murmured, kissing Cullen. "I really had a good time."

"I did too. Thank you, as well," Cullen murmured, then he paused and wrinkled his nose. "Do you smell that?" Coughing a little, Emlen nodded. "Yeah, bleach and stuff." She looked around and then cried out as she darted around the short wall to where the table and the mess surrounding it lay. "Oh, my gods, Cullen! Someone's been in here."

Crouching down, she reached for some of the papers as Cullen grabbed for her arm. "No, Emlen, don't touch it! Step back and open a couple of windows to get the fumes out. I'll call the police."

As she stumbled back, Emlen turned for the windows and began opening them, coughing as the fumes choked her. She spied Barnabas out on the porch and went to get him food to put outside. She didn't want him inside with the fumes and mess.

There were a lot of questions from the police as to why the damaged files included police files. Cullen used his ex-cop connections with the boys in blue and told them they were his old files for a case Emlen was helping him research. They dusted for prints, took their statements and left the two of them to clean up the mess.

By the time they'd got the worst of the mess cleaned up, the reality of the situation had hit them both. Emlen poured them each a whiskey and sat down, hands shaking as she realized how violated she felt.

"I'm sorry all the information was damaged and that we could only save a few things," Cullen offered, voice low. "It's really going to set back the investigation."

It took a minute for Emlen to process what he said and then she grinned a little, shaking her head. "No, we're fine. I scanned everything over the past few days and uploaded it to my private cloud server. While having the actual files to look at can be helpful, we didn't lose anything."

"But someone thinks we did," Cullen said and grinned back at her before he lifted his glass in a toast. "Nicely done, Emlen. This gives us an advantage now."

"How do you think? Because they figure we're handicapped now and we're not?"

"Exactly. Every little advantage is in our favor." Cullen drained his glass and pushed to his feet. "I'll go through the house and check it one last time and then I've got a beach to clean up. Try and get some sleep, Em. There's a cruiser sitting on the house tonight. You're safe."

Emlen could hear him going through the house, checking windows and doors, opening closets and so on, making sure there were truly no more surprises in store.

She really wanted to take a shower but settled for brushing and braiding her hair and washing her face before she stepped out into the kitchen that still bore a faint scent of bleach and put the kettle on. A cup of tea would help calm her before sleep and she could use some calming right now.

"Emlen! You got a key for this door?" Cullen called out and for a moment, Emlen couldn't think what door was locked before remembering the attic. "Yeah, I do, but you don't need to check up there. It's fine." Emlen called back and chewed her lower lip. She didn't want to open that door any time soon and she really didn't want Cullen to see what was up there. Not before she had a chance to see it all and deal with whatever emotions opening it brought to life. Pouring her tea, she cupped her hands around the mug and leaned back against the counter, watching as Cullen came into the kitchen.

"No, I need to check it. I'm surprised the cops didn't when they were here. Give me the key so I can make sure it's okay."

"No, Cullen, you don't need to check it. It's still locked, right?"

"Yes, but so was your door when you got home. Doesn't mean someone didn't get in now, does it?" Sarcasm made the words short as he folded his arms, giving her what she was calling his 'intimidating cop look'.

That look waved every red flag in Emlen's arsenal and she drew a slow breath before glaring back at him. "And it's none of your business, or anyone else's business, what is behind that door. Let it go, Cullen."

"Emlen...he could be hiding up there."

"And he could be gone. I'll take that chance. I'm not opening that door."

"You're being unreasonable, you know that, right?"

"Then I'm unreasonable. You can leave anytime now. Thanks for your help. Goodnight, Cullen."

"Emlen..." Cullen sighed and reached out a hand to touch her arm, and she backed up. "Emlen, come on. What's behind that door, anyway?"

"My mother's things, things from when we lived here. I was told your parents boxed it all up and put it in the attic. I looked in there once when I first moved back and then locked it up again."

"So, let me check it out. I won't go through boxes or anything, just make sure that asshole isn't up there, hiding."

"I appreciate it, but no. I'll check it out myself later. Seriously, I will," she replied. "But I'm not opening it for you. It is something I need to do it myself."

"You're being stubborn, Emlen."

"Yep." A sip of her tea hid her smile. She looked up at him through her lashes. "Go home, Cullen."

Shaking his head, Cullen stepped up and kissed her forehead, then headed out the door. "Lock up behind me, woman!" he called out.

Emlen set down her mug and went to the door to lock it behind him. Turning back, she pulled the attic key out of her pocket, rubbing her thumb over it as she headed for the stairs. Pausing by the front door, she pulled out the drawer in the credenza and took out a Glock 9mm, checking to make sure there was a round in the chamber before she went up the steps to the attic door. Heart pounding, Emlen held her breath as she carefully turned the key in the lock. The gun aimed at the opening, she gently nudged the door wide. Right hand holding the gun, her left reached in and slid up the wall to hit the switch, bathing the attic space in the yellow glow of two bare bulbs. Using the training she'd gained from her bodyguards, she swept the room, clearing it of any possible hidden person.

Not finding a living soul in the cluttered space, Em tucked the gun into the back of her pants and started really looking through the room. Boxes, bits of furniture, old lamps, a large basket full of her baby toys. Her fingers toyed with the hair of what had once been her favorite doll, one her mother had got for her that looked like her - auburn hair and violet eyes. The memories washed over her and she closed her eyes, taking a slow breath, filling her lungs with the scent of vanilla musk. Turning, she pulled a box marked 'clothes' towards her and pulled off the top, the scent of the perfume growing stronger. A silk scarf lay on top and she lifted it, pressing it to her nose and breathing in the faded scent of perfume. "Mom's perfume," she murmured, finally placing that fragrance that had been haunting her since she came back. Looping the scarf around her neck, she looked in the box a little more before closing it and setting it aside.

The one underneath it was marked 'photo albums' so she picked it up and headed out of the room, shutting off the light, but leaving the door open. She'd faced what was up there and now it was time to air the space out a bit. Cullen may have thought she was being stubborn but going up there was ripping off a bandage. She didn't know what she would find or how emotional it would make her. Showing emotion meant showing weakness and she didn't know him that well yet. Laying the gun on her nightstand, Emlen sat with the box on her bed and opened it, taking out the plastic baggie of loose photos and the three albums tucked inside. Rubbing her hands together, then rubbing them over her face, she took a moment to calm herself.

Picking up the one covered in faded pink silk with "E.B." in embossed gold letters on the cover above a cherub holding flowers. "My baby book," she murmured, opening to the first page. Her name, date of birth, weight and length, the hospital she'd been born in and what time were all on the page. Ink prints of her hands and feet were there too. The next page had been torn out, but the edge of the page closest to the binding was enough to show it would have listed her parents. "Moth..." and "Fat." were all that were left of the page.

"Guess she didn't want me to know that," she muttered to herself and turned the page again. A photo of her as a baby was there, held in what were clearly a man's hands. Pulling the book closer to the light, she examined the picture and noticed what seemed like part of a tattoo on the inside of the man's left arm. She knew her grandfather and uncle didn't have any tattoos, so this had to be her father. "My first clue." She grinned.

Getting to her feet, she carried the book into the kitchen, digging in a drawer to find the magnifying glass she had stuck there after going over the police file photos. Turning the overhead light on, she held the book up and used the glass to really examine the image. "Damn, I can't tell what it is a tattoo of. Maybe a bird?" A groan and she lay the book on the counter, then started turning more pages to see if there was another image of the man. Nothing. "Dammit!" She tossed the glass on the counter and folded her arms, starting to pace back and forth. "I need to know what that tattoo is!"

"It's an eagle." The voice soft, barely a whisper, as the fragrance grew stronger.

"What?" Emlen asked, spinning around in a circle, thinking there was a person nearby. She knew, deep down, there was no one *living* there. "What did you say? Who is it?" Her fingers pressed to her lips and she whispered, "Mom? Is that you?"

"The tattoo. It is an eagle. Blue album," the voice whispered back and then the scent faded.

"Blue album," Emlen murmured, then turned and raced into the bedroom. She pulled the blue album off her bed, flipping it open. She didn't even question that she'd just gained a clue from her dead mother's ghost. "Aha!" she called out, pulling a photo free from the page. Another one of a man holding her when she was about a year old, but only from the neck down. A full image of the tattoo was in the photo - and it was an eagle with 'semper fi' in a banner clutched in its talons. "A Marine tattoo. Well, now we're getting somewhere." Pulling her phone out, she started snapping photos of the images, then texted the two to Cullen with a message "look what I found!' Taking a few minutes more, considering how the other stuff had been damaged, she took photos of all of the pages of all of the albums and uploaded them to her cloud storage. A yawn hit her hard enough to make her ears pop and she shook her head, stacked the albums back in the box and tucked it under the edge of her bed.

Falling into bed, she stretched and pulled a pillow to her chest before closing her eyes. She was going to sleep with a light on tonight.

12

Remembrance: Chapter Eleven

Cullen didn't see the texts until morning, and it took a second cup of coffee before the import of the texts registered. "Holy shit," he yelled and jumped to his feet, staring at his phone. "That has to be her father. No bloody face, but that tat..." he hit a button and called his brother. "Mornin', Connor."

"Morning, Cull. What do ya need?" Connor replied.

"Can't I just be calling to say hello to my little brother?"

"Sure. Hello. Now whatcha want?" He sounded irritated and more than a little stressed.

"Easy, Conn. I've been helping Uncle Joel with some research and I found a photo of a tattoo, I was wondering if you could run it through the database for me?"

Connor sighed and Cullen heard the desk chair creak as Connor leaned back. "Yeah, okay. Send it over and I'll..." a faint 'ting' signaled a message coming in on Connor's phone and he laughed. "...yeah, I got it. Okay, I'll see what I can find and get back to you."

"And Connor..." Cullen added, voice low. "...keep it on the down-low. We don't want anyone knowing about the photo or that we're looking into things on this old case. A woman's life depends on it."

"A woman's...wait. What case is this, Cull?"

"The Brewster murder," Cullen said.

Silence met his words for a good minute before Connor spoke. "She's back in town?"

"Yeah, back at the old place," Cullen replied.

"I'll come by your place tonight?" Connor asked. "I'll bring the results by."

"Sounds like a plan. See you tonight." Cullen hung up the phone laying it on the table. Now to see if he could get Emlen to agree to the plan to bring his brother in on the case. He leaned back and sipped his coffee, gaze drifting to the view of the ocean beyond his window. He'd finished up the last construction job almost two weeks ahead of schedule and it was a good thing since he needed this time now to help Emlen. He had trouble thinking about anything else these days and with the break-in at her house last night, his worry for her had increased tenfold. It had taken him a while to fall asleep because he kept getting up and checking out the windows to see if anyone was creeping around her house; to see if the cruiser was still sitting guard; to see if there was anything to worry about. He felt a little sorry for her, noticing the light in her room had been on all night - not that he blamed her for that in the least. Finishing his coffee, he put the mug in the sink and then grinned, remembering he still had her little cooler to return after cleaning up the beach picnic last night. Stepping out onto the porch, he stuffed his feet into his sneakers and picked up the cooler before he jogged down the steps towards her place. Knocking on the door, he glanced over to where the cruiser still sat and waved at the officers inside before turning to smile at Emlen as she opened the door.

"Good morning. I brought your cooler back and wanted to chat." Emlen had apparently just finished dressing after a shower and the light purple tank top and denim shorts looked cool and comfortable, her damp hair braided out of the way.

"Morning, Cullen. Come on in. Coffee should be done, and we've got some stuff to go over."

His gaze was on her butt as he sets the cooler down near the back door and followed her into the kitchen. "Do you have any paper cups? Those guys outside could probably use some coffee."

"Already handled, along with some muffins from that bakery on Main. I bought a bunch yesterday morning. They were quite appreciative." Emlen grinned at him and poured two mugs, handing him one. "So, you got my texts from last night?" She led him from the kitchen into the living room and curled up on the couch, the box of photo albums sitting on the coffee table.

"Yeah, so you think that's your Dad?"

"I'm pretty sure it is. None of the photos have his face, though. The only lead we've got is the tattoo and the fact he was in New York and Boston between the time I was born and when I was about two. That's when he is no longer in the photos. It was about a year later that Mom moved us here."

"It's not a standard Marine Corps tattoo - looks custom, so I did something you might not be happy with..." Cullen started to speak, then glanced up at her. "I told Connor you were here when I asked him to run the photo of the tat through the database."

"Are you serious?" Emlen gasped, staring at him. "What part of 'don't tell anyone' did you miss? Even Joel said to not tell anyone else. If it was okay to tell Connor, don't you think he would've said it was?"

"Joel probably figured I'd already told Connor. I mean, we tell each other practically everything. Always have. Besides, we don't have access to that database and Connor does. We need his help. And no, this doesn't compromise him as a cop either, because it's a cold case and you're not a suspect or anything."

"Gee, that's comforting," Emlen muttered and sipped her coffee. "Well, it's done now. How long do we have to wait to hear from him?"

"Would you like to come over for dinner tonight? Steaks on the grill, a couple of sides, some beer…" Cullen asked.

"And a chance to talk to your brother about his findings, assuming he gets any?" Emlen gave him a wry laugh and shook her head. "I guess so. I'll bring some potato salad or something." She nodded towards the box. "Take a look. My baby album and a couple of other photo albums, and a plastic baggie full of loose photos. I've been through all of them and scanned them up to the cloud, and I didn't see any more of the tat or of any that could be that guy." Cullen put down his coffee and pulled the box to him, taking out the baby album first and slowly flipping through it.

"Whoever your father was, your Mom was really angry with him if she all but erased him from this," he murmured after a few minutes of looking.

"Yeah, I got that impression too," Emlen replied, sipping her coffee and watching Cullen's face as he looked through the album.

A frown furrowed his brow and he flipped back and forth between a few pages and then pulled out his phone and typed something.

"What're you looking up?" "Someone looked familiar and I'm trying to see if I'm right or just imagining things," Cullen said.

Leaning over, Emlen looked at his phone and then the photos. "Oh, that's Uncle J.C. He's not really a blood uncle, but a friend of my grandparents. Judge Jackson."

Cullen looked up at her and then back at the photos. "Senator Jackson's father?"

"Wait, his son is a senator?" Emlen asked, then shook her head. "The guy always made me feel really uncomfortable. Like one of those creepy uncles that you avoid because he keeps trying to get you to sit on his lap."

"Yeah, his son, John F. Jackson is one of the senators from Massachusetts," Cullen replied. "And most recently, the Vice Presidential candidate on Hugh Bannerman's ticket."

"I'm not surprised that someone with those kinds of connections is tied to my grandparents," Emlen offered. "They've hosted Kennedy and Shriver events at their Boston townhouse. They have strategically placed photos of themselves with several US Presidents and celebrities around the house. It's kind of nauseating, honestly."

"Nauseating?" Cullen asked, laughing a little at her choice of words.

"Yeah, because they're assholes with a false sense of grandeur. Sure, there's money in the family that goes back a couple of generations. Most of it came from my great-great-grandmother's family when they escaped Europe during World War I. Sure, we've got the Brewster name and ties to the Mayflower, but so do hundreds of thousands of other average, every day poor people."

"My mom says that we're descended from a couple of the Mayflower families too. I can't remember, she does that genealogy stuff now that she's retired." Cullen leaned back with his coffee. "So, Connor is running the tattoo through the Tatt-C database and we'll see if something comes up. Maybe it will narrow down the field of people to consider. Also, CSI didn't find any prints other than yours, mine and the last couple of tenants in this place, so no leads on who broke in last night."

"I've been thinking about that. I don't think they came here just to mess with the files, because the only ones that knew about them were you, Joel and me. Unless you told someone else?" Her tone shifted to slightly accusatory as she eyed him over the rim of her cup.

"I didn't tell Connor until this morning and he's the only one I've spoken to about any of this since we got the boxes from Joel."

"I'm wondering if maybe someone figured out who I am, in spite of the disguise and all. It's not like I have really worked hard at hiding - just doing my usual 'not being blatant' tactic. So, maybe someone saw me and saw that I was living here and put two and two together."

Cullen reached for a photo in the album and pulled it free. "Well, it could be someone who really knew your Mom too, because you look a lot like her. See?" He handed her the photo and watched her reaction.

"Yeah, I didn't realize how much we looked alike until last night. There are no photos of my mother at my grandparents' house or at my aunt's place either. It's like they tried to erase her from the family or something."

"Your coloring is different. Her hair is blonde and her eyes blue, but your features are a lot like hers. Someone wouldn't have to work hard to put together that you're her daughter."

"And yet again, we haven't narrowed down anything because we've been all over town and I've even gone out to Provincetown a couple of times, so it could be anyone from anywhere." Emlen sighed and rubbed a hand over her face. "Wait...did you tell Joel about the break in last night? I feel so bad, all those hard copies destroyed after so many years of being safe."

"No, let me call him and make sure he's okay," Cullen replied and pulled out his phone. "Hey, Uncle Joel, give me a call. It's important." Glancing over at Emlen, he sighed, "Voicemail."

Emlen's fingers toyed with the mug for a few moments then put it down. "I may not be a cop, but I'm getting a weird feeling. Can we take a ride over and check on him?"

"A weird feeling?" Cullen asked, setting his own mug down. "Well, there was a lot of Joel's information in those files, including his current address. I was going over the files in my cloud, matching things up with photos and realized how much of his information was in there. That means whoever trashed my place..."

"...has his information," Cullen finished and got to his feet. "Get your shoes and lock up, let's go." He jogged to the door and out, heading up to his place to grab his keys, wallet and truck. Didn't take him more than three minutes before he was pulling up in front of Emlen's house.

As she climbed into the truck, he called out to the cops sitting on the house. "Hey guys, we need to go run an errand. Keep an eye on the place and we'll be back within an hour, all right?" They nodded, waved and Cullen's truck tore down the drive. Fifteen minutes later, they pulled up in front of Joel's, the truck barely shut off before they ran up onto the porch.

"Joel! JOEL!" Emlen called out as she got to the door.

She went to grab the handle and Cullen grabbed her hand. "No, Emlen, don't touch it." He pulled his gun out of the holster tucked in the back of his jeans and tugged her to stand against the side of the door, back to the solid wall of the house. He kept his gaze on the door and asked, "Look to the docks, do you see his boat?"

"Yes, it's there," Emlen murmured, face pale. "We need to go inside, Cull." The sure knowledge that something was horribly wrong hit Emlen in waves, making her breath hitch and her body shake. The only other time she'd felt like this had been when she was nine. Whatever was behind that door, she was certain it was bad.

Cullen gave her a nod then gestured for her to stay put as he carefully opened the door. The inside door was open about an inch and he used the tip of his gun to nudge the door wider. "Uncle Joel?" he called out before stepping inside. He could smell the coppery tang of blood about three paces inside. The room had been ransacked, so Cullen walked carefully through the debris as he cleared the space, making sure the perpetrators were no longer there. Stepping around the wall that separated the living area from the kitchen, he found Joel's body on the floor.

"Emlen, call 911 and get the cops here," he called back. "And do not come inside, it's a crime scene." He could hear her choked gasp and then the sound of her making the call as he crouched down beside Joel's body.

No pulse, not that he expected to find one. The chef's knife from the block spilled over on the counter was firmly planted in Joel's chest. "I'm so sorry, Uncle Joel," he whispered. "We'll find whoever did this. I promise." Then he got to his feet and carefully checked the other rooms, not touching anything, before he made his way back outside to Emlen.

"He's dead," he said, voice cracking. "Someone trashed the place and stabbed him."

"Oh, Cullen. I'm so sorry!" Emlen choked out and then turned to him, hugging him tight. Tears streamed down her cheeks. "Whoever did this...it's because of me. I know it."

"We don't know that," Cullen said as he put an arm around her, patting her back lightly, the other hand still holding his gun. "It's probable, but remember, Joel was a cop for nearly thirty-five years. He made a lot of enemies. It could have been any one of them."

Pushing back, Emlen glared up at him. "Are you serious right now? What are the chances of that? He was living here, retired, for what, six years? And no one had bothered him - until we show up and stir up this fucking mess and now, he's dead?" She pushed at his chest and whirled, arms wrapping around herself as she stomped over to the porch railing.

"No wonder you're not a cop anymore. Even I am not that clueless!"

Stiffening at the painful words she threw at him, Cullen hissed low and grabbed her arm. "Don't say things about something you know nothing about, woman. I chose to stop being a cop and it's none of your business why. Now get your ass back in the truck and head back to your place. You can't be here when the cops come. Having you tied to this will blow any hope of keeping your identity under the radar."

Emlen nearly slapped him when he grabbed her arm, but then she saw the pain in his face and heard the truth in his words. Instead of flailing him verbally, she jerked her arm out of his grip and stomped towards the truck. "Try and explain why I made the 911 call then, genius," she yelled back as she got in and started the truck. She wasn't gentle in her handling of it as she turned around and spit gravel on her way back down the road, not even bothering with adjusting the seat or putting on her belt until she got to the main road into town.

Pulling the truck into Cullen's drive, she got out, threw his keys into the mailbox on the fence post and jogged back to her house. The watch car was gone and Emlen didn't even notice as she unlocked her door and stomped inside, slamming the door behind her.

"OH, that infuriating, pig-headed asshole of a man!" She kicked off her shoes hard enough to bounce one off the wall and stomped into the kitchen, proceeding to take out her frustration on the few dishes left in the sink from breakfast. Before she knew it, the dishes were done, the cabinets organized, and all of the counters and appliances wiped down.

With a fresh pot of coffee brewed, she poured a cup and went out to the back deck, still pacing but a lot calmer than when she got home. Sure, she realized that she had reacted badly - poor Cullen just lost someone he considered family - but he also had treated her like a liability and an incompetent woman, and that was not the kind of treatment Emlen would ever accept from anyone, ever again. She'd let herself fall back into that kind of acceptance with Brad, and it infuriated her that she'd slid into it with him after working so hard to become strong and independent outside of her family's connections. It was very likely, she thought to herself, that Cullen had just become the target of a mix of that residual anger, the fresh fear, and worry about the current situation. "I'm such a fucking mess," she muttered and leaned against the railing to watch the waves and sip her coffee.

She'd found, about three days after moving here, that staring at the water did have some calming effect on her, and Emlen could really use that calm right now. A good ten minutes passed before Emlen realized tears were streaming down her cheeks. Another person had died because of her family's messed up history.

Joel had been kind and honest and had really tried to find the answers over the past twenty years. It wasn't fair. She dropped into one of the padded chairs and tucked her legs up, fingers still clutching the mug. It was something solid, warm and tangible - an anchor for the whirlwind of thoughts and fears that seemed to have caught her up in its onslaught and pulled her free of her moorings.

That's how Cullen found her, sobbing in near silence, gaze on the cove and fingers clutched around a mug holding the dregs of cold coffee. He had shown up, angry, grief-stricken, and worried, and when she didn't answer the knock on the door, he'd walked around the house and found her on the deck. Without a word, he walked up to her, tugged the mug from her fingers and scooped her up in his arms, turning to sit on the chaise with her in his lap. Silent still, he wrapped one arm around her, hand on her hip, the other stroking her hair as she buried her head against his shoulder. Holding her like this, the panic and fear he'd been dealing with soon faded into the more productive emotions of grief and anger.

"I shouldn't have sent you away. I'm sorry," he finally muttered into her hair.

"I get it," Emlen whispered. "I was really angry and hurt at first, but I get it." Fingers lifted to wipe at her cheeks, and she sniffed before looking up at him. "I'm so sorry about Joel."

"Me too." He sighed and looked down at her tear-stained face, her eyes looking bluer today due to the contacts she was wearing. "They're calling it a 'home invasion' murder, but I learned a few things that I want to share with you and Connor later. I'm almost convinced this was tied to your mom's murder case and those files."

"Shit, I forgot about Connor." Emlen squirmed out of his lap and rubbed her hands through her hair. "Crap. I need to clean up and get the potatoes going and..."

Cullen reached out to catch one of her hands and tug her closer. "Easy, Emlen. He's going to pick up some sides and I have the steaks already. Just go grab your shoes and whatever, lock up and we'll go to my place."

A faint smile and she leaned over to give him a brief kiss. "All right. I've got dessert in the fridge. I can bring that. Give me five minutes and I'll be ready."

Cullen watched her grab the mug and head inside, the heel of his hand rubbing at his chest. That woman was getting to him in ways that he'd never experienced before. He wasn't quite sure what to make of it. The rush of pleasure he felt when he saw her coming towards him. The fear and panic he'd felt more than once, thinking she was in danger. The heat that flooded him whenever she kissed him. There had been hints of one or the other of those emotions with other women he had dated, but never all of them, and never to the degree he was feeling them now. And there it was again, that pleasure and anticipation at the first sight of her walking towards him, face washed, hair freshly braided and changed into jeans instead of the shorts. She was beautiful, brilliant and she was going to be his. Holding out his hand to take the container from her, he asked, "You lock everything up?"

"Yep, all locked up and my new laptop and a few things are locked in the back of my Rover, just in case." Emlen tucked the keys into a front pocket, the phone into a back one and she looped an arm through Cullen's. "Don't tip that, it's blueberry cobbler," she chided as he almost bobbled the container at the feel of her pressing close. "So, tell me about Connor. He's a Mass State police officer now? Trooper or...?"

"He was a trooper, now he's a detective. He's really good at the job and he loves it. I'd been working with Dad in his contractor business when Connor started talking about going to the academy. He and I both got undergrad degrees in Criminal Justice. I had considered going on to law school, but that was about the time Dad started really needing help with the business. His arthritis was making it hard to function in the cold weather and it started impacting his work. Connor had just graduated and applied to the academy - and talked me into dropping an application too. I did, because I really wanted to be a cop, but I also had to do what I could for Dad. When he saw we both wanted it, he chose to retire to Florida with Mom and settle for doing cabinetry and woodworking in his little shop down there. Best thing they could've done was move into the warmer weather."

They stepped up onto Cullen's deck and Emlen set the dessert container down on the table before turning to look up at him. "It's getting late. Want me to get the dishes and stuff together while you get the grill started?" She bit her lip for a moment and opened her mouth as if to say more but closed it, pressing her lips together in a line.

He'd fully expected her to dig and he was sort of ready to share the story with her, but the reprieve was welcome. "Sure, go grab the stuff and I'll get this lit and warming. Oh, and can you get the stock pot and half-fill it with water? Connor's bringing corn on the cob and we can quick boil it."

Emlen nodded and went to get her share of the tasks done while Cullen managed his. She really loved his house and the way he'd mixed old and new to make it efficient and comfortable, yet rich with heritage. Filling the stock pot with water, she watched him get the grill set up and lit, admiring the fit of his jeans as he bent to adjust something. He really was not her usual man type, but she was realizing that her 'usual' was not as adept at stirring her as Cullen was. Then again, her 'usual' type was really good at making her hate men. Lifting the pot, she headed for the door, using her backside to push it open before stepping out and nearly colliding with Connor as he jogged up on the deck.

"Woah!" she gasped as he grabbed the pot in a reflexive move to keep it from falling. "I'm sorry, I wasn't looking."

Connor's eyes widened as he looked at Emlen and he shook his head. "No, my fault. Wow, I can't believe you're really here." He grinned, but the smile wasn't very bright or enthusiastic. "Let me get that," he said as he took the pot and turned to hand it to Cullen. "All yours, big brother."

"Gee, thanks," Cullen smirked at his sibling before setting it on the flame and then eyed Connor's empty hands. "Where's the stuff?"

A thumb jabbed back over his shoulder. "In the SUV. I was coming to get help to unload."

Emlen started walking towards the driveway. "Well, let's go get it. I'm starving." she called to them as she moved away.

Connor put a hand on Cullen's shoulder and leaned in, voice low. "Damn, but she looks a lot like her mother."

"Yeah, wait until you see some of the photos she found." Cull replied and nudged Connor with his shoulder. "Come on, I don't like her being out of sight for too long."

13

Remembrance: Chapter Twelve

Food was cooking, chips, pickles, and other nibbles were set out on the table. The three sat with beers in hand, snacking while they waited for the steaks and corn to be done.

"So, before we talk about Joel, I wanted to share what I learned from the database," Connor started, setting his beer down and pulling a thumb drive out of his pocket. "This has some of the data that seemed most relevant on it, but before I hand it over, you need to promise that you will never say where it came from or how you got it."

"Agreed. Journalistic protection of sources is still mostly supported by the courts - and if they really push, I'll just tell them I found it on the beach." Emlen smiled and reached for the drive. "So, what is your analysis of the data?"

Cullen rose to turn the steaks and glanced back at his brother. "I told her you were good at the detective stuff, so don't make a liar out of me," he teased and tended the grill while Connor spoke.

"There were only seven or eight tattoos in the database that were similar to the one in your photo, but none of those were identical. Yet, they used the same coloring and stylized line work, so they are highly likely to be from the same artist - a guy who runs a studio over on Comm Ave named Iggy Zapata. I figure we could take a run up there with the photo and see if you can get him to spill.

Granted, it's been about twenty years, but Iggy is still sharp as a tack and while his boys do most of the work, he still does pieces now and then."

"I don't think I've ever heard the name, but yes, let's go see if he remembers anything helpful," Emlen said, sipping at her beer. "I'm sorry that stirring all this up got your Uncle Joel killed, guys. I can't help but feel responsible for all of this."

"Wait, Emlen. This is not on you," Cullen told her, taking the steaks from the grill and putting the plate on the table, then getting the corn before sitting down. He started to serve the food while talking. "I said I wanted to share this with you both, and it sucks saying it at all, so I'd rather just say it once. While I waited for the locals and CSI to show up at Joel's, I checked out his hidey holes and found a few things that made their way into my pockets." He pulled out one of those purse-sized photo albums, a worn envelope, and a couple of keys on a two-inch plastic lobster key ring. Setting the keys on the table, he passed the envelope to Connor and the photo album to Emlen. "From what I have put together so far, Joel had been working the case off and on since it happened. He'd take a break for a few months, then dive back in."

Connor opened the envelope and found what appeared to be pages referring to financial records of more than one or two people of interest. "Uncle Joel always did say to 'follow the money' - looks like he was doing just that."

"And it looks like he was friendly with my grandfather," Emlen whispered, turning the book to show them a photo of Joel and her Grandpa Brewster on Joel's fishing boat. "There are a few of them together here, and one of Joel in a tux at some event with my grandparents on either side of him." She slid the book back over to Cullen and Connor, then started to cut her steak and begin to eat with a calm precision.

"Any idea what these keys are?" Connor asked his brother.

"One is clearly a safe deposit box, but I'm not sure what the other is. It looks old." Cullen replied, handing the keys over. He started to drop them, Connor grabbed for them, and the plastic lobster broke in half, revealing a USB drive. "Well, maybe the answers are closer than we thought?" he said as Connor stared at the keys and the drive in his hand.

"Where's your laptop?" Connor asked.

"After food, guys," Emlen replied. "And before you plug that in, make sure you turn off the Wi-Fi, so no one has access to what you're looking at."

Both men looked at her in surprise, then Cullen grinned. "See? I told you she was a smart one."

"You'd make a good detective," Connor added, tucking the keys into his shirt pocket before digging into the food.

"Between the lessons I got from my bodyguards, the training I did to be an investigative reporter, supplemented with pieces from a couple of cop friends, I have a nice mix of disciplines to pull from."

"I've also told her we're going to hit the range this week," Cullen added. "She already knows how to shoot, but it's been a couple of months, right?"

"Yeah," Emlen replied. "Almost four months now. I started going again after I got rid of Brad, but before I moved here. I had about a month of travel to finish up my last assignment."

"Let me know when you guys are going. I can always use more range time," Connor said, "And we can see who the better shot is." His gaze darted to his brother and he nudged him with an elbow. "You haven't beat me in almost two years. I know you've been practicing more, so let's see if it's helped?"

Cullen took a slow sip of his beer and eyed his brother. "You volunteering to bring the targets?" "You betcha." Connor laughed as Emlen looked confused.

"What am I missing?"

"We liked to bring...uh...interesting targets. Like small watermelons, water bottles, creative paper targets and so on, Connor answered her.

"Creative paper targets?" Emlen asked. "Uh huh. Zombies or werewolves or vampires or robots... things like that. Makes it more fun," Cullen told her, taking another bite of food.

"I was always told that using human-shaped targets was a reminder of what we'd most likely be shooting at if we were ever in a situation, so it was a good idea to stay with the norm." Emlen leaned back, taking a sip of her beer and watched their expressions.

Connor spoke first. "That's true, but there are plenty of incidents where what you need to shoot is an elbow or a shoulder, when a perp is hiding behind something." "Or someone," Cullen added, voice quiet. "That's when it helps to have had practice shooting at other things. It helps your eye and mind train on seeing the potential target over the object as a whole. Just consider it thinking outside the box'." Connor smiled as he took a sip of his beer adding, "Besides, it's fun to watch the little watermelons blow up."

Connor was doing what he could to lighten the mood before Cullen dropped fully into 'that' place. He hadn't had those dark moments as often the past couple of years, but it still could happen, and Connor was on reflex mode to keep it from happening in front of Emlen. It was pretty clear to him that his brother's improved mood, demeanor, whatever you want to call it, had gone up by an order of magnitude since Emlen had come back into town. His 'white knight' complex would suffer if he 'went dark' in front of her. So... Connor to the rescue.

"You guys ever see the musical Into The Woods? There's a line where the witch goes "Boom...squiiiish!" and it replays in my head when I get to shoot something that goes boom." Emlen chuckled. "One of the guards, Rory, he had been with me when I saw the musical and then about a month later, was on duty when I was at the range. We were shooting at water balloons and I kept going 'boom...squish' and he got laughing so hard, he dropped the water balloon he was tying off and it started a water balloon fight among the four of us." Emlen was grinning, eyes shining bright as she told the story. "One of my better memories." She toyed with the beer bottle in front of her and glanced up at the two men. "So, when we shoot watermelons, I get to yell 'boom...squish!', agreed?" Both Cullen and Connor were laughing as she lifted her beer bottle to toast them as they nodded in agreement.

"And who's bringing the water balloons?" Cullen teased, shaking his head. It had been a long time since he'd appeared this lighthearted, even with all the horrible stuff that had happened over the past few days.

"I will." Emlen called out, raising her bottle in salute and laughing. "Be prepared to LOSE!" she crowed before settling back in her seat. "Okay, I'm stuffed. I'll clear the dishes if one of you makes some coffee and grabs the laptop? I want to see what's on that drive before the three of us leave tonight. I get the feeling that it's going to be worth our sobering up a bit." Rising, she started collecting plates and bowls, and headed into the kitchen.

The guys could hear her in there, wrapping up food and running water, so Connor leaned over to his brother and murmured, "I'm worried about what we'll find on here. The photos of her grandparents with Joel mean there is some sort of deeper connection and she didn't even dig into it. Just set it aside."

"I've noticed that with her. Anything that deals with her grandparents or aunt is kept at arm's length or tucked away. I get that she is focused on her mother and what happened, but from what I've gathered about her life afterwards, this wasn't some random home invasion or whatever you want to call it." Cullen slowly got to his feet and leaned closer to Connor. "I think the only reason she's still alive is because she didn't remember. I also think that now that she's digging, she's a target once more, and that Joel's murder was a part of this whole mess and not some other case as the investigators have told the news."

"I agree," Connor replied, also getting to his feet. "I'll bring in the last couple of things here. You go get your laptop? I'll get coffee going while I'm in there."

Cullen nodded, reaching out to grip his brother's shoulder as he followed him into the house.

Coffee, pie, and the laptop with the Wi-Fi shut off lay spread around on Cullen's dining room table. They'd decided it would be smarter to be inside, away from potentially prying eyes, as they went over the new information. All three of them agreed they had a new level of paranoia where the cold case was concerned. Cullen sat in front of the laptop, waiting as the program checked the drive for viruses before opening the folders. Connor leaned over his shoulder and Emlen paced back and forth behind them both.

A soft 'huh' from Connor had her leaning over Cullen's other shoulder. "What? What's on it?" Emlen asked.

Folders and documents spilled across the screen as the drive opened and showed its contents. "Looks like a mix of things. Some copies of the files he gave us, some new stuff. Photos, newspaper articles..." Cullen paused and clicked on a folder. "Emlen...look."

The folder was filled with copies of every article ever written by or about Emlen - even the ones where she used her Baldwin byline to keep some anonymity with the more heated pieces.

"Holy shit," she whispered, reaching over to use the touchpad on the laptop to scroll down and see the full contents of the folder. "Even my high-school paper stuff is here. Did Joel do this, or did someone give it to him? Any way to tell?"

"Maybe, but it'll take some time," Cullen replied.

Connor nodded, adding, "It's possible, but without the right programs, there's no definitive way of telling."

Emlen pointed at a folder. "Can we look at the photos? See if they're the same as the little album or if there are more there?" Cullen clicked back to the folders and opened the photo one, setting it to large thumbnails so they could be seen as a whole.

"Looks like more fishing ones with your grandfather, some event photos - maybe the same as the ones in the album, and..." he paused and clicked on one, and it filled the screen. A photo of Emlen as a toddler with her mother...and Joel. "Wait...what?" Emlen gasped, sitting in the chair next to Cullen and leaning in to look at the image. "Does this look like what I think it looks like?" Her gaze went from the image to Cullen and Connor.

"You mean, does it look like your mom and Joel were more than friends? Yeah, it does," Connor replied.

"He didn't seem to react to me as if there was more going on, when we saw him a few days ago, right?" Em asked, gaze going to Cullen.

"Maybe he did, and we just considered it the reaction to seeing you and going over the case files?" Cullen toyed with his mug, thinking about the last conversation he'd had with Joel, the night before he was killed. "There was something worrying him, though. I spoke to him the night before he was killed, and he seemed off."

"What did he say?" Connor and Emlen both asked at the same time, then chuckled a little before looking back at Cullen.

"He said that the torch was being passed to me but didn't specify what torch. I assumed he meant watching over Em and helping her with the case. Then he apologized for the burden he was putting on my shoulders. He asked me if I remembered all the niches and hidey holes in his house - which is why I went through them all before CSI and the cops got there, Cullen said.

"I think we need to ask Dad if there was something going on with Joel and Camille," Connor offered, voice soft. "I'll ask him, so he doesn't think you're diving back into the case, Cull. We don't need him getting pissed about it or anything."

Emlen felt like she was missing something, but she held her tongue and just watched the brothers. There was obviously something they were avoiding discussing and she could feel the truth in the words they spoke to each other. Love, pain, regret, strength and determination echoed in the words and resonated within her. "Instead of making copies of that drive, how about we make a cloud account under a false name and load it there, then all three of us can access it as needed?" Emlen offered after a moment.

"Maybe let Connor stash the drive itself somewhere safe, since my house has already been hit once and with Cullen around and next door, his place would be too easy a target."

"Good idea," Cullen replied and smiled at her while Connor started typing again. "John Smith has a new cloud account. The password is 'Joel' with a three where the 'e' belongs, and an exclamation point at the end," Connor spoke after a few moments. "The files are uploading now."

Cullen started to clear up the last of the dishes and poured more coffee as the three settled back at the table. "I'm supposed to get a call today about when they'll release Joel's body. He wanted a stone at the cemetery with some of his ashes there and the rest scattered in the harbor."

The mood sobered a bit as they sipped coffee. "I wish I'd been able to get to know him better," Em murmured. "He seemed like a really cool person. Interesting, and educated, and experienced..."

Cullen laughed. "He was, easily, one of the most intelligent people I had the pleasure to know. He read all kinds of books. Everything from Louis L'Amour westerns to presidential biographies and books on the Templars and medieval history."

"He even had a whole library dedicated to the occult and supernatural. Horowitz's Occult in America and a worn copy of Malleus Maleficarum," Connor offered. "He always seemed like such a hard-facts, cold-logic type of cop that his having all of that made me ask him about it once."

Em quirked a brow at Connor in encouragement while Cullen snorted soft laughter into his own cup. "I bet that went well," Cull muttered, still chuckling.

"About as well as you'd expect," Connor replied with a grin.

"He told me that I should read more Shakespeare, because even the Bard knew that 'There are more things in heaven and earth', as Hamlet stated. That what we now call science and technology was once considered the realm of magic and mysticism. That we needed to educate ourselves so that we didn't only know things but understood that we did not know things."

"Sounds like one of my college professors," Em replied and leaned back, setting down her mug. "Okay, I don't know about you two, but I'm starting to feel the food coma. Thanks for the great meal, but I'm going to head home." She rose and started to gather her things.

"I've got an early morning tomorrow," Connor said and closed the laptop. "Still training for the marathon and need to run off this meal." He smiled and moved to give Emlen a hug. "It was so damned good to see you, Emlen. Don't disappear on us again, okay?"

Em hugged him back. "Don't plan on it, big brother. See you on the range soon, yeah?"

Connor nodded and reached out to fist-bump Cullen. "See you soon, brother. Stay safe."

"You too," Cull replied, and watched his brother leave before turning to Em. "Let me walk you home?"

"It's only a few yards, Cullen." Em shook her head. "But sure, I'd like the company."

Cullen paused and tucked the laptop under the cushion of a nearby chair and grabbed his keys, heading out with Em and locking the door behind them. "Never bothered with locking up much unless I was getting in my truck and going somewhere. Now? Now I lock the damned door if I'm walking down to the beach. It's crazy."

"I'm sorry for bringing that to your door," Emlen offered, her voice sad. "I feel responsible."

Cullen stopped and turned, tugging her gently to face him. "This is not on you, Em. Not even a little bit. This is on whomever murdered your Mom and Joel, and whoever is trying to terrorize us now. Which, by the way, I think is all the same person or group of people. This is not random, and it is not new." His hand lifted to tuck a fluttering strand of her hair behind her ear and Cullen cupped her cheek. "Don't let them make you feel anything you don't want to feel, okay?"

A faint smile curled Em's lip. "I can't wait to meet your mother again. She did a good job with you two, if you can say things like that and actually mean it."

"I've gotta admit, not telling my folks you're back has been tough. They talk about you even now, and it would make them so happy to know you're doing well and back home."

"Well, maybe when we get through this, we can take a trip to Florida and see them? I'd like to thank them for what they did back then."

"Yes, let's do that!" Cullen pulled her in for a quick kiss, laughing low as he hugged her.

Emlen caught her breath with the kiss, eyes closing as she leaned into him. "Damn, do that again?" Em gave a nervous laugh as she lifted her chin to meet his lips once more. She slid her hands up to rest behind his shoulders, feeling his muscles ripple under her palms. Her lips parted and the heat coiled low in her belly.

A low groan from Cull as he kissed her, then lifted his lips. "We keep doing this and the seagulls are gonna get a show. How about we go inside?"

Em could see the desire in his eyes, but he'd been doing a great job of not pushing beyond her comfort zone. For the most part. Cull's question was like a splash of ice water and Emlen shivered, catching her breath and taking a step back. "As much as my body is screaming at me to do just that, I try to use my head first and I'm still not willing to make you a rebound. That's not fair to you or me."

"Does it help if I say I don't care?" Cullen grumbled. "I don't feel like a rebound guy, and you have to admit there's some pretty intense chemistry here."

"It helps - but it doesn't change my mind," Em replied. "I want to make sure I don't fuck this up like I have every other relationship I've been in." She turned and took his hand, starting to walk again towards her house.

"From what you've told me, it was Brad that screwed it up by cheating on you."

"Yeah, but why did he cheat? Was it because I wasn't available enough? Too..." Em stopped and let out a breath. "Until I'm feeling better about it, it's best to not rush things. That's all."

"Too...what?" Cullen asked, stepping up to take her keys and unlock the door. "You stopped mid-sentence there."

"Eh, nothing really. He just never stayed the night with me because of my nightmares. Said he needed his sleep too much." "Oh, for pete's...what an ass." Cullen huffed as he closed the door behind them and turned to her. "That's on him, Emlen, not on you. What if holding you in his arms would have quieted the nightmares and kept them away? Did he ever even try?"

A shake of her head no, and Emlen turned to set the container on the counter, hands pressed to the cool surface.

Arms wrapped around her from behind, and Cullen whispered into her hair near her ear. "Maybe we can try that sometime? I'm willing to sacrifice sleep if it helps you get through this. That's what people do when they truly care about someone else. They sacrifice. They support and encourage, too - which is why I'm going to encourage you to go grab your laptop like I know you're wanting to do and dig into the cloud files while I take a quick walk around your place for my own peace of mind." He stepped back and winked at her before turning to walk out of the room.

Emlen smiled as she watched him walk away and called out, "The upstairs is unlocked now. Feel free to check it, too." She grabbed her keys and stepped out to her Rover, pulling her laptop bag out of the covered cargo hold. Em was back inside at the table before he finished his rounds.

"House is clear - and if you want, I'll come help drag some of those boxes out of the attic for you to go through when you're ready. Looks like some cool stuff up there."

"I'd like that," Em replied, eyes on the screen as she started opening files. "Maybe in a couple of days? I want to see if there are any more photos or journals or anything up there."

"Sounds like a plan," he said as he moved over to press a kiss to the top of her head. "I'll leave you to work. Message me if you find anything good, otherwise I'll see you." Cullen headed for the door and paused. "I'll lock it up, but come hit the deadbolts, okay?"

"Yep..." Em called out, not even looking away from the files.

He chuckled as he stepped out and tugged the door firmly behind him. Stretching, he gazed out at the water and then back at the house. Having her here was better than he could have hoped. He actually enjoyed life even more with her around.

14

Remembrance: Chapter Thirteen

It had been almost two weeks since the cookout at Cullen's place, and all three had been messaging bits of what they were learning about the files. Tonight, they were gathering at Emlen's to go through some of the boxes from the attic. Em and Cullen had brought down several, and there had been a few trips to the thrift shop to drop off items no longer needed or of no real sentimental value. Em had filled a small box and taken it over to Cullen's, to see if his parents wanted some of the things.

Emlen pulled into the drive and shut off the vehicle, taking a moment to enjoy the cooling breeze. The weather had warmed up as the days had crept into summer and she was never more grateful for the seaside location than right now. Her head felt full of the scattered puzzle pieces that, on their own, were intriguing enough but had not yet come together to make any real sense or any larger picture. They were missing something, and she hoped the boxes held some answers. Gathering up the grocery bags, Em headed inside and started unpacking. She'd bought fresh rolls and sandwich fixings, some prepared salads and a package of chicken wings that just needed heating. Finger food had been decided, so they could eat while they worked and not waste any time.

Cullen had stacked the boxes around the living room yesterday so they could be more systematic. With the windows open, a breeze flowed through the house, chasing away the musty, dusty smells that had followed the boxes down from the attic. Wings in the oven, the rest of the food set out on the counter, Emlen pulled out her laptop and phone, and prepared to add to the cloud database they were compiling. A knock on the door had her glancing over to see Connor standing there, bags in his hands.

"Come on in, it's open." she yelled, and moved to reach for one of the bags as he nudged the door open with his foot.

"Hey Em, nice to see you again. I brought some beer and some of that flavored water stuff you like, and a couple of bags of chips. Cull said you were doing sandwiches and stuff, so I thought it'd help." Connor set the bags on the counter and pulled out items to put in the fridge.

"Thanks, Connor. I figure we'll be running late so extra snacks are always good." Em grinned at him and moved to give him a hug just as Cullen walked in.

"Hey, no making moves on my girl, Cullen growled, laughing as his brother jumped back about a foot.

"Jeezus, Cull, you gave me a heart attack! Warn a guy when you're going to go all alpha dog on him, will ya?" Connor teased, nodding to the fridge. "Might as well add yours to the ones I just brought. Beer for days, I guess."

"Or just enough beer to keep you two working until we're done?" Emlen replied, laughing as she leaned over to kiss Cullen's cheek and then gestured to the food. "Let's get our plates fixed and get started. I pulled out my laptop and phone so I can scan anything we find right to the cloud. Not taking any chances after the last fiasco."

"Sounds like a good idea to me," Connor replied around a mouthful of chips as he started to fill his plate.

Laughter and light chatter filled the room as the three got food and drinks, and settled around the living room, taking a few minutes to eat before starting.

"So, what did you guys find when you brought the boxes down?" Connor asked, swallowing a mouthful of sandwich. "A lot of vintage clothes," Emlen replied dryly. "And stuff for a household back then. Took the whole lot of it to the thrift store for them to sort and deal with."

Cullen nodded and nudged a box with his foot. "This one has a lot of books, but it may have more than just novels in it. I'm hoping anyway." He reached over and flipped the lid open and yelped, jerking back as Barnabus leaped out of the box and stretched before padding over to sniff at a pickle that had fallen from Cull's plate.

Emlen's laughter filled the room, hand cupped in front of her mouth as she worked to swallow while laughing, tears in her eyes. "I should've figured. Cat and boxes go together."

Connor was snorting laughter as well, then picked a bite of chicken meat off his plate and held it out. "Here kitty..."

"His name is Barnabus. He showed up here the day I moved in, and knew just where the cat food was, so I named him," Emlen replied, wiping her face with a napkin and eyeing Cullen's glare as he picked salad off his lap and cleaned up the mess from nearly dropping his plate when the cat surprised him.

"Bet he tastes good with soy sauce," Cullen muttered, then started to chuckle. "That was funny though. Damned thing nearly gave me a heart attack."

"No, you're not cooking my cat," Emlen retorted and watched the grey tabby head over to Connor and nibble delicately at the offering before ripping it from his fingers and darting under the coffee table.

"See? You scared him," she admonished Cullen, trying to look stern and dissolving into laughter once more. Barnabus settled under the table, enjoying his treat and ignoring the humans laughing. Emlen put her plate to the side and reached for the box nearest her, pulling it open and taking a few of the items out. "This one is books and papers, looks like a couple of my Mom's journals." She paused and glanced up at the brothers. "I'd like to ask that if you come across any of her journals or diaries, that I get to see them first?"

"Of course," Cullen replied, and Connor nodded, mouth full still. Or again. It was hard to tell.

As soon as one box was emptied, it became the repository for all things deemed not useful and the coffee table was becoming covered with papers, loose photos, framed photos and journals. "Three...four...five...Wow, Mom wrote a lot," Emlen murmured, trying to put the journal pile into some semblance of chronological order.

"My mom keeps journals too," Cullen offered, not looking up from the book he was flipping through. He went through each book since earlier he'd dropped one and found a few loose photos falling out.

"Yeah, she has them stacked in file boxes in the closet," Connor replied. "I tried reading them once. She made sure I never even considered it again. He winced in remembrance and glanced at Cullen.

"Don't look at me, I never even tried. I saw you not sitting for a couple of days and didn't even think about it." Cullen grinned and set the book aside, reaching for another. "Didn't she leave a couple of boxes of them at your place?" Connor asked.

"Yeah, they're up in the attic in a plastic tote bin. I moved them out of the box when I put them up there so they wouldn't get damaged. And no, I still didn't look at them."

"Such willpower," Emlen teased before reaching for another box. "About two more boxes and we're done. The rest of the stuff upstairs is furniture and a few things that I wanted to keep of Mom's. I took her jewelry to the shop to be cleaned and repaired, but for now, this is all that's left." The three fell silent as they worked their way through the last bit.

After about an hour, Connor leaned back and looked around the room. "I'll get us some more drinks and then Cull and I can move these wherever you want them, Em."

"Those books over there, I want to keep. The rest of the stuff can go. We've pulled all of the personal stuff out so it's just books and magazines left. The papers that have no real value we can throw out. I just didn't want to risk tossing something important until we'd gone through it." The brothers started settling the 'to go' stuff into boxes and sealing them up, carrying them out to Cullen's truck while Emlen cleared the plates and lunch food, and set out bowls of snacks and fresh drinks that Connor had put on the counter. Sorting the remainder into piles, she settled down with the journals, picking through them until she found the ones that would have been from around the time of her conception. A shiver ran through her and she let out a breath. "Mom? I hope you don't mind me looking at these. We need answers now more than ever."

A faint caress brushed her cheek and she let out a sigh before opening the notebook. It was leather bound with a band that wound around it top to bottom to hold it closed. She took a minute to appreciate her mother's beautiful script and then started to read. She didn't even look up when the brothers returned and started on their own piles, getting lost in the story.

It's been three days since the gala, and I can't get him out of my mind. It's like I finally saw him after knowing him all these years. The way he smiled, the way he moved - it was like I was seeing a stranger. Then he asked me to dance and it was as if we were made for each other. We're supposed to go out tonight and I've nearly emptied my closet, trying to find the right thing to wear. He says to dress to impress, so I will. Who knew that the boy I saw every summer, would grow up to be so incredible? Emlen let out a breath. "I think I found where she met my father, but she's not said a name yet."

"Oh, wow. Keep reading," Connor encouraged, turning over another paper from the pile in his lap. "I've got a bunch of financial stuff here, but nothing that looks like it'll help us. I'll sort it for you to go over later if you want."

"Sounds good..." Emlen replied, voice trailing off as she kept reading. Cullen watched her face, the play of emotions as she read the pages and nearly forgot to pay attention to his own pile of sorted documents. It took his breath away, how beautiful she was.

Connor reached over, not even looking at him, and swatted his arm. "Back to work." he muttered, grinning. "You can stare later."

Four months since we danced at the gala. Three months since we 'danced' at his apartment and I know now, with certainty, I'm pregnant. I'm afraid to tell him. He's usually a gentleman and kind with me, but he's been talking a lot about his dreams and aspirations and I don't think he sees me as a part of that future. I don't think -I- see me as a part of that future. A politician's wife? Ending up like my mother and grandmother? That is the last thing I want, nor the kind of life I want for my child.

Emlen's breath hitched and she flipped through the pages, skimming quickly.

It took me two weeks to get up the nerve, or find the right time, whatever excuse you want to use - to tell him about the baby. He was excited at first, then fearful. He's worried about telling his parents, particularly his father, and their reaction. He wants to get married, but I don't know if that's what I want. It's not the late 1800's but the late 1900's and a woman doesn't have to be married to have a child anymore. I don't know what I'll do if he asks.

Well, at least he wanted me. Em thought to herself as she kept going.

We're not going to tell anyone for a bit now. It's easy enough to hide with loose shirts and dresses, but after Tina's death, his mom isn't handling things well at all. She spends her days and nights in a Valium and booze haze.

Emlen looked up. "Did Judge Jackson have a daughter?"

Cullen stopped and looked at her in confusion while Connor pulled out his phone and started searching. "Yeah, Valentina. She died when she was nineteen in a drunk driving accident."

Em let out a slow breath. "Uncle JC is my grandfather, not my 'uncle'. John Jackson is my father."

"How do you know?" Cullen asked.

Connor just watched as Emlen glanced down at the journal in her lap. She took a breath and read the last bit to them, then looked up at the brothers. "She was about four months pregnant with me at the time."

Connor turned back to his phone and nodded. "That would fit the timeline too. Holy shit, Em..."

Cullen's expression shifted to determined and angry. "So, which is it, then? Is the Judge trying to kill you or his son?"

Emlen's face paled and she let out a breath. "I'll keep reading. Right now, he seems to have wanted me - the son that is. Mom was unsure about marrying him if he asked her, about being a politician's wife. She didn't want the same kind of life for me that she'd had with her parents."

"Your Brewster grandparents weren't politicians though, right?" Connor asked.

"No, but they might as well have been. They were high society and counted many politicians and other famous people in their circle. They were in the news and papers all the time. Anything that happened in the family became instant fodder. It's why they sent me off to boarding school as soon as I was old enough to go to school. If they'd had boarding schools for toddlers, I probably would have been in one then."

Cullen jerked to his feet, tossing the papers he'd been going through onto the chair and started pacing.

Connor glanced up at his brother, then turned to Emlen. "Emlen, it pisses me off that they treated you like that, and I'm sure that's part of what has Cull so furious. We've talked about it before; how different life would have been if you'd stayed in our house and been our sister."

Cullen gave Emlen a wry grin. "Well, that would have made a few things rather awkward now, if we'd been raised siblings, wouldn't it?"

A soft chuckle and she nodded. "Creepy if I were attracted to my brother," Em replied and leaned back. "I probably wouldn't have the issues I have with relationships and abandonment if I'd been raised with you guys. You're both good men and I can tell your parents did a good job. I'm curious though, why my father's name isn't on my birth certificate and why he never claimed me - or why my mom's family never gave me to him. They sure as hell didn't want me. My aunt gave the twins, my cousins, anything they wanted - but I was the one that had to perform to standards in order to get anything. I was a duty, never a pleasure. Luckily, Uncle Jonathan was a kinder man and showed me some love and affection. Well, he did whenever Aunt Corinne wasn't around."

"Cousins?" Connor asked. "Oh...right, the Hale twins. They're all over the media. Used to be for their antics and mischief, now it's for who their dating or what club they've been seen in. I forgot they were your cousins."

"Yeah, we have never been close. They were taught early that I was about the same level as a servant's child, never to be considered family," Em told him before opening the book again, her finger having marked the page. "Let me see what more I can learn."

Cullen huffed out a breath. "I need some air. I'll be back in a few minutes." Em glanced up as he headed out to the porch, gaze flicking to Connor.

He rose and gave her a wry smile. "I'll make sure he doesn't punch something." He moved to follow his brother. As soon as they stepped out, Emlen started reading once more.

15

Remembrance: Chapter Fourteen

Frankie sat in his old Ford van, eyes on the house a few yards away. He'd been watching the lights in the windows, waiting for the girl to go to sleep. He had his thermos of coffee, bag of jerky and a whole pound of sunflower seeds to keep him going, as well as three cans of chewing tobacco. He could sit here all night and planned on it if he had to. The boss had been pissed that he'd not taken the girl out yet. It was supposed to have been done over a week ago, but his van had been in the shop part of that time and it was his busy season at the bait hut.

Frankie's fingers lifted to lightly touch the bruise under his eye. The message sent by the boss had been real clear though. He didn't care if Frankie lost business or had to bike to do the job. It had to get done - and now. So, here he sat, spit bottle in hand, and eyes on the lights in the windows. He sat up and pulled out the binoculars when the two figures walked out on the deck. A low laugh rumbled in his chest as he saw the brothers leaning against the railing.

The boss didn't care about the brothers – but Frankie had always hated the O'Brien boys. Always thought they were better than everyone else.

One looked pissed, the other looked not pissed. Frankie wasn't sure if he was excited or frustrated, the way he bounced a foot on the deck and stood with his arms crossed. Didn't matter much. If he could take out all three at once? The boss would probably give him a damned bonus!

Shifting in his seat, he glanced behind the passenger's seat and reached to pull the tarp a little further over the crate sitting there. In it were six bottles of lamp oil with wicks poked through the caps and plastic wrap snugged around them for safety. He probably wouldn't need that much, but it was better to be safe than sorry with the boss up his ass. Was also why he was using chewing tobacco tonight and not smoking it. He didn't want to blow his own ass up because he did something stupid.

Settling back, he spit into the bottle again and looked over at the brothers on the deck. Yep, this was going to be a good night.

16

Remembrance: Chapter Fifteen

Cullen jerked when Connor came out and put a hand on his shoulder. "Not now, Con. I need to just walk this off a bit."

"I get it, but maybe talk it out first? What's got you all twisted up?"

"Which part? The fact her family are a bunch of shits? The fact that if it is her father or her grandfather going after her - the chances of us stopping them are slim to none?" Cullen turned to glare at his brother. "Do you really think we could take on a Vice Presidential candidate or a sitting Federal judge and win?"

"Easily? No," Connor replied. "But I'd put money on it that the reason they're going after her now is because of the coming election. Jackson and Bannerman are running a ticket on family values. Having an illegitimate child show up, tied to a wealthy donor family, would cause all kinds of trouble."

"Having that child killed and her identity splashed across the media would cause even more trouble, don't you think?" Cullen snarled.

"Only if that information got out. It's looking pretty good that her family knew exactly who her father was and that had a lot to do with why they kept her buried in boarding schools."

Cullen slapped a hand against the deck railing and leaned against it, back to his brother as he gazed out at the beach and the water beyond. "They'd never tell, even if the fuckers murdered her. Their reputation and social standing are too important."

"Yep. So, we need to get the information out before they do," Connor replied.

Now Cullen understood why his brother was so calm. He'd already figured out the best way to play it. "Damn." He turned and looked at his brother, his smile slowly growing. "You've already got the answer." Stepping up, he pulled Connor into a hug, then slapped his shoulder. "Let's head inside and see what Emlen says."

Connor stopped walking, pulling his brother to a stop. "Wait. Let's not lay it out for her yet. She's dealing with a lot of emotional shit right now, reading those journals. We don't need to spin her emotions any higher until she's had a chance to process. We'll just do our part and then see what she wants from there."

A nod from Cullen and he let his shoulders relax. "Yeah, you're right. We don't need to overwhelm her any more than she is right now."

Stepping inside, Cullen went to press a kiss to Emlen's temple while Connor grabbed the coffee pot and a couple of fresh bottles of beer. "How are you, Emmy?" Cull murmured as she glanced up at the kiss.

"It's a lot, but I'm getting a lot of answers." Em's hand lifted and she cupped his cheek. "Thanks for asking. I'll be fine. Really."

He turned to kiss the palm of her hand and then dropped down to sit, scooping up the other journals and holding them in his lap. "I'm going to put all of these others in a bag and tuck them in your Rover with the other stuff. Want me to put your laptop in there too?"

Em nodded and then paused, "Take that baggie of photos too. I didn't get them scanned yet and I don't want to lose anything."

"Got it." Cull replied and pushed to his feet, gathering everything up and tucking it all in the messenger bag. He turned toward the door when a 'whoosh' and a crash had him spinning around. Emlen shot to her feet. "What the hell was that?" was all she got out before the smoke detector in the front of the house went off. Another 'whoosh' and crash and Connor yelled from the kitchen, running into the room, eyes wide. "Get out of the house! It's on fire!" He grabbed a box and tossed it out the door onto the porch, not even paying attention to what he was grabbing.

"Forget that!" Cullen yelled. "Em, grab your phone, let's go!" He shouldered the bag, grabbed his keys and phone and took her hand, tugging her to the back door.

They'd just reached it when another crash had the room behind them exploding into flames. Connor grabbed at them and pulled them with him towards the deck, coughing as the smoke billowed out around them.

Shoving Emlen's keys at his brother, Cullen yelled "Get her Rover away from the house!"

Connor raced off into the smoke while Emlen stared at the flames in shock, the journal she'd been reading, dangling from her hand. Cullen tugged on Em's arm, pulling her off the porch and away from the rapidly burning house, trying to dial 911 on his phone at the same time. "Fire at Rocky Cove road!" he coughed. "Everyone's out of the house but it's going fast!"

They stumbled down the steps and over to the rocks near the beach, Emlen still seeming in shock as he led her to a spot far enough away to clear the air when he heard a 'pop' and suddenly he wasn't holding her arm any more. Cullen turned just as he heard another pop and felt a searing pain in his leg, dropping to a

knee before he saw Emlen lying on the ground, not moving. "SHOOTER!" he
shouted before he flattened out and reached for her neck, trying to find a pulse.
It was there, but her shirt was wet and sticky and in the flickering firelight it was
hard to tell where she'd been hit. "CONNOR! SHOOTER!" he yelled again
before reaching for his ankle holster, the pain in his thigh shooting its own kind
of flames up his spine.

Connor had just got out of the Rover, leaving it at Cullen's house, when he
heard a shout. He couldn't make out the words, but he grabbed his own gun
and raced along the edge of the lighted area, staying in the shadows as much as
possible. He heard the second shout clearly and dropped even lower, eyes
skimming the area to try and see where a shooter might be. Not wanting to give
the shooter a bead on his location, he pursed his lips into the bird whistle he
and Cull had used when playing in the woods as kids. He saw Cullen's head lift
and turn, then heard the distinctive snap of a bullet hitting rock just as Cull's
head dropped back down and he started crawling backwards, pulling a still
Emlen with him. "Shit," Connor hissed, his gaze moving to where the muzzle
flash showed him the location of the shooter. He dropped down off the ledge to
the sand and raced around the curve of the beach, hoping to come up behind
whoever it was and surprise them.

The sirens from the fire department ripped through the air as the burning
cottage shot flames and shattering glass around the yard. The noise worked in
Connor's favor as he managed to get back up the ridge and come in behind
where he'd seen the muzzle flash. He was just hoping the shooter hadn't moved
into circling him instead. Nearly convinced that he'd overshot the spot, Connor
nearly stumbled over the man, slamming himself into a tree before he gave
himself away. The bulky figure rose to his feet, a sniper rifle in one hand, the
other holding binoculars as he scanned the area where Cullen and Emlen had
been. Cursing, the figure dropped the lenses to bounce against his chest as he
lifted the rifle again and started forward. Connor moved quickly and pressed his
9mm against the man's head and snarled, "Drop it, right now."

Frankie froze. The rifle slid from his fingers and clattered on the ground as his hands slowly lifted to about shoulder height. "Don't shoot. I was just comin' to see if anyone needed help."

"With a sniper rifle? I don't think so," Connor snarled as he used his free hand to pat the guy down. "Lock your fingers behind your head and get on your knees."

"No," Frankie replied, voice calm.

"What do you mean, no? DO IT!" Connor snapped and grabbed the back of Frankie's shirt collar, jerking him backwards to get him to drop.

"You ain't gonna shoot me and I'm not going to let you arrest me," Frankie said before his right hand dropped to his necklace and then into his mouth almost before Connor realized what was happening.

Foam spilled from between Frankie's lips and his eyes rolled back as his body shuddered and hit the ground. Connor sidestepped out of the way of the falling body as the poison took the man's life within seconds.

Crouching beside Frankie's body, Connor patted him down and grabbed the keys and a cell phone, stuffing them into his own pockets before he holstered his own gun and moved away from the body. He came back up from the beach closer to where he'd last seen Cullen, moving fast as he spotted paramedics lifting Emlen onto a stretcher and another pair trying to get Cullen onto another one.

"Stop fighting them, Cull. Get up there," Connor said as he approached the group, his attention on his brother first.

Cullen's gaze went to his brother's face and Connor just gave a faint shake of his head to tell him to not ask as he moved closer.

"How bad?" Connor asked.

"Em's hit in the back and I got a graze on my thigh. Bleeding like crazy but I'll be fine," Cullen replied as Connor leaned in and whispered.

"Dead. Talk later."

Cullen nodded and called out, "Get the bag, would ya?" before he let the paramedics strap him in as they wheeled him up the lawn. The firefighters were already hosing down the remains of the cottage and Connor's gaze slid from the wreckage of the home to the two being slid into an ambulance. "I'll meet you there," he called out to his brother and then walked up towards Cullen's place, trying to look casual as he pulled out his keys. Snagging the bag from the ground, he found the journal Emlen had been reading and stuffed it into the bag with the others, locking the whole thing in his car before he took the rest of the stuff out of her trunk and secured it as well. Locking her Rover, he put the keys in Cullen's house. Taking a few minutes to wash up and borrow a shirt from his brother, Connor was soon on his way to the hospital. On the drive, he called Dave Cook, the sheriff who took over when Joel retired. "Dave, it's Connor O'Brien. My brother and his neighbor were shot, and her house was torched. The guy that did it - his body is to the left of the house in the brush. I was about to arrest him when he ate what I think was a cyanide pill. I'm on my way to the hospital to check on my family, but I'll be available for questioning after."

Dave sighed. "Jeezus, Connor. Who was the guy? Are you okay? Is Cullen going to be...?" Connor cut him off.

"Cull is going to be fine. I'm worried about the neighbor. But the guy? I think he was Frankie Kyle, the bait shop owner."

"Frankie Kyle shot two people?" Dave sounded stunned. "What the actual fuck?"

"I think he also torched the house with kerosene bombs. And took poison to avoid being arrested." Connor's voice caught and he let out a breath. "I'll tell you what I can later. I'm pulling up at the hospital now."

"Okay, Connor. I'll be up after securing the scene. Call me if you leave there," Dave replied.

"Will do, Sheriff. Stay safe. I don't know if Frankie was alone."

"Got it." Dave hung up and Connor tucked his phone away. He parked as close to the ER as he could and made sure to be in clear view of the traffic of people and vehicles and under the lights. If anyone was going to mess with his car too, he wanted a lot of witnesses. Stepping into the ER, he pulled his badge as he headed up to the counter. "Cullen O'Brien and Emlen Brewster," he stated. "Where are they?" A few moments later, a nurse led Connor back to where Cullen sat on a gurney, another nurse bandaging his leg.

"Em's in surgery," Connor told his brother. "How're you doing?"

The nurse finished taping the bandage in place and told Cullen to wait for the doctor before she cleaned up the supplies and stepped away. Ash, dirt and blood covered Cullen and he glanced at Connor's shirt. "Did you bring one for me?" "No, didn't think about it. I was busy getting everything out of Em's Rover to lock it up in mine. Your house is locked up too," Connor replied. "I'll find you some scrubs or something in a minute. Did you hear anything?"

Cullen shook his head and shifted position, looking down at his cut open pants leg and the bandage around his thigh. "They gave me something for the pain. It's making me foggy." Connor nodded, then grabbed a basin and stepped away, coming back with warm water and a few things to help clean Cullen up. By the time he returned, Cull was leaned back against the raised bed, eyes closed.

"I'm gonna clean you up a bit," Connor offered gruffly and proceeded to wipe some of the mess off of his brother's face.

Cullen lifted a hand as if to stop him and Connor shoved it down. "Just let me do this." He took a rough breath and then added quietly. "Please."

While he cleaned, he spoke in a low murmur. "Cook is taking care of the shooter's body, the fire department was still working on the fire, and Emlen's in surgery. That's all I know so far. I'll have to go give Dave a statement later, but I wanted to make sure you guys were okay."

"Did you kill him?" Cullen asked.

"No, he killed himself. It was Frankie Kyle."

"The bait guy? What the hell, Connor?"

"I know, right? But he had some kind of old saint's medal around his neck and when I tried to get him to kneel, he grabbed it and stuck it in his mouth. A few seconds later, he was dying. Looked like cyanide, but I'm no coroner."

"Why would the town drunk and bait shop owner have cyanide? For that matter, why would he have a sniper rifle and be firebombing a house?" Cullen asked, opening his eyes and looking at his brother. He reached for the washcloth and took it upon himself to finish cleaning up.

"All good questions." He nodded to Cull's leg. "So, how bad is it?"

"Twenty-something stitches. It was a graze, but it went deep enough to need 'em. Good thing I'm not the one doing a marathon soon, eh?" Cullen set the cloth aside and dried off, then looked around.

"Doc is supposed to be bringing me a script for pain, but I really want to know how Em is."

"Me too," Connor replied. "Let me see if I can learn something." He stepped out and flashed his badge again a few times before coming back in. Cullen sat in a wheelchair, good foot tapping restlessly. "The bullet went through her side, about mid-back at an angle. Missed everything important but they'll be a while stitching everything up and making sure," Connor reported. "We can wait outside of surgery if you want."

Cullen nodded and Connor grabbed the chair, pushing him towards the elevator. "You get your prescription?"

"Yeah, it's gonna be filled here and I can pick it up on the way out," Cullen replied. "Let's go wait for our girl, huh?"

Connor chuckled. "Our girl. I like that." His smile faded as he slid the chair into the elevator and hit the button. "Seems the further we get into this, the fewer answers we have instead of more."

"And the more players we uncover. At least we saved those journals. I think they're going to be the key to this whole thing." Cullen spoke low as the elevator dinged and they rolled out into the hall. "I also think it's time we told the folks what is going on. Can't hide all of this from them and it's best they hear it before it hits the news."

"I'll call them in the morning, Connor told him as they settled in the waiting room, letting the staff know they were there for Emlen. "You good here for a few? I'll get us some coffee and call Dave. I want to see if he can hold the report for a bit."

Cullen nodded and leaned back, closing his eyes. All Cullen could see against his closed eyelids was Emlen lying on the ground, the flames of her home raging behind her. He was glad she would be okay, but wrapping his mind around the fact that the town loser had been the one trying to take her out? Frankie had been around since he was a little kid and was a good twenty years older or more than Cullen.

Had he been the one to take out Camille? The real question - on whose orders? Frankie just didn't seem to have the brain power to coordinate a long-term task like this. Did he kill Joel? Too many loose threads... His thoughts were interrupted by a warm paper cup being pressed into his hand. Eyes opening, he saw his brother's worried face. "Thanks," he mumbled as he lifted the cup to sip.

"It's only a step above cop shop coffee," Connor warned as he sipped his own, dropping into the chair closest to his brother. "Dave says they got the body and the fire is out. FD is watching for hot spots and taking samples." Cradling the cup in his hands, he stared into it for a moment before looking around the empty room and then back at his brother. "I took his keys and cell phone. Pulled the sim card while on the phone with Dave. I'll see what I can find on my own before finding them in the brush later."

"That's a huge risk, Connor." He stared at his brother, eyes wide. "You don't want to lose your job over this."

"They tried to take out my brother and the woman I look on as a sister. I'll take the risk. Oh...and Dave agreed to hold the report for at least twenty-four if not forty-eight hours. Give me time to call the folks and see what I can find."

"Is he going to get you the results of the coroner's report?"

"He said he'd let me know what the poison was if it was a poison. I know for a fact it was a poison - nothing else acts that quickly. The foam on his mouth makes me think cyanide, but Dave said he'd let me know for sure."

"What about your statement?"

"I gave it to him over the phone. I'll swing by the station on the way home, read it over and sign it. It doesn't say much. We were hanging out after dinner and someone firebombed the house. I moved the Rover away, and someone shot at you and Em. I went after him, being a cop and all, and he offed himself by biting his necklace." Connor shrugged and sipped at his coffee. "Lunatic drunk doing something insane. That's what they'll try and feed the news if more than just a fire comes out. So far, the shooting is being kept quiet, and you and Em are here as a result of the fire, nothing more."

"Dave learned from the best. I'm glad he's on our side," Cullen offered, voice low. The painkillers the doctor had given him earlier were starting to really kick in and even the coffee wasn't keeping his head upright. "Con, I'm about to crash. Help me onto that sofa thing over there and I'll just rest until we get some news."

Once he got Cullen settled, asleep even before he managed to sit in a chair nearby, Connor pulled out his phone and started researching. He remembered Frankie from when he was a kid, always drunk and belligerent to everyone. His folks had warned them away from the bully and they'd managed to never get on his radar, unlike some of the other boys in town. He found the old news article and then skipped to the database to look up the police report.

Frankie had been brought in for questioning on the disappearance of Tommy Lanahan. Tommy had been somewhere between Connor's age and Frankie's - a recent high school graduate when he'd disappeared just before Christmas. They'd found his body the next spring when a lobster trap had brought up a hand. The divers had gone in and found the kid chained to a couple of cinder blocks and dropped in the harbor. Frankie had been brought in because the two had been seen arguing outside the mini mart just before Tommy disappeared. No evidence could point to it, but the detective on the case wrote that he still thought Frankie had something to do with it. "Yeah, I do too. Now," Connor muttered as he read.

A nurse stepped in and looked at Cullen, sleeping, then turned to Connor. "Detective, you here about Miss Brewster?"

He rose and nodded, keeping his voice low. "I am. My brother needed rest." he gestured and then turned back to her.

"She is out of surgery and in recovery. It'll be a while, but once we have her settled in a room, I'll come get you so you can go see her. Everything went well, according to the surgeon."

A soft breath of relief slipped from him and Connor smiled. "Excellent news. Thank you."

She turned and walked away while Connor ran his hands through his hair and sprawled next to Cullen again. The day was catching up to him, so he folded his hands over his belly and leaned back, letting his eyes drift shut.

17

Remembrance: Chapter Sixteen

Emlen felt like she'd been walking forever. All she could see around her was fog, and all she could hear was the faint sound of dripping and an odd wheezing. Bone weary, she just wanted to find a place to rest, but nothing seemed safe and there were no places to sit if she stopped. She couldn't remember how she had come to be in this place or what she had been doing before she started walking. It felt like she had always been walking. Her body ached and she looked down at herself wearing jeans and a t-shirt but barefoot. Muck all over, her arms and hands filthy. The stench of wet ash and mud filled her nose and she stopped in the middle of the path, trying to wipe her hands on her shirt. Now that the sound of her own steps had been silenced, she could hear a faint murmur of voices. "Hello? Is someone there?" Emlen called out, the words seeming to be swallowed up by the fog, not carrying much past the little clear space the fog had left around her. Turning in a circle, she tried to pinpoint where the voices were coming from, but it seemed to shift directions and never sounded very clear. Scrubbing her hands on her jeans once more, she started walking again.

"Emlen." A voice called out to her and Em stopped, turning slowly.

She spied a figure in the swirling fog and tipped her head, staring at it as it approached. "Emlen," it said again.

She sucked in a breath. "Mom?"

"Yes, Emmy," the figure replied, a smile in her voice as she finally stepped out of the mist and into the ring of clear space around Emlen.

Em stared at the figure in front of her. The similarities between them were clear - as were the differences. Little details that faded photos just couldn't share. Emlen's coloring - her nose curled up slightly at the tip and her mom's was perfectly straight. Her ears were smaller than her mom's. She pulled on the hem of her shirt and stepped closer, the vanilla fragrance washing over her, and she closed her eyes, breath catching on a sob. "Oh, Mom..." as Camille took that last step and wrapped her arms around her daughter.

The hug lasted for a few moments, but it would never be long enough for Em. "Mom...why are you here? Where are we? I remember a fire..." her voice trailed off and her eyes widened. "Wait...am I dead?"

"No, Emmy. But you're unconscious after surgery. Your mental barriers are down enough for me to come to you. We really need to talk."

"Yeah, we do. There's a lot you never told me, Mom. Not as a child, or later, when you would come visit." Em's tone was accusatory as she folded her arms under her breasts.

"You were three when I was killed, Emlen. You weren't old enough to understand. As for later? The amount of energy it takes to break through is immense and doesn't give me a lot of time to get messages across. It's not like email, you know."

"No, Mom, I don't know. That's the problem!" Emlen's voice rose as her frustration flooded her. "I don't know anything! I have no one to ask!"

"You could ask your father," Cami answered her, voice soft. "You know who he is now."

"Do I really? I don't even know if we're really having this discussion. It's probably some morphine-induced hallucination."

"JJ is your father. He knows who you are - but he cannot acknowledge you - for your safety as well as his own."

"What do you mean?" Em asked, eyes wide.

"The Order would be after you in a heartbeat. Ask your Garda about it."

"My what? What's a Garda?"

"You need to be more aware of what you do to others, Emlen. You race into situations with no consideration of the harm it does to others. Susan Clark is still having problems because of the memories you invoked. Daryl Simmons is now an alcoholic and is still unemployed because the information he gave you could only have come from him and he paid the price."

"I'm an investigative reporter, Mom. It's part of the job. Those are what we call 'acceptable risks'," Emlen retorted.

"Your gifts mean you have a greater responsibility towards the betterment of all. Not an excuse to abuse them and manipulate situations so you benefit," Cami replied, her voice calm but strict. Typical mom tone when correcting a child.

"What gifts? I have had to fight for everything I've gained, Mom. You've no idea." Emlen turned away from her mother, anger surging through her again. The whooshing sound grew louder and then faded, a faint beeping filtering in through the fog.

"You have gifts, Emlen. Blessings or curses, depending on how you use them. It's time for you to go back now. Just remember this - it's your responsibility to use the gifts wisely, or the price you pay will be too high. I love you, daughter. To the moon and ba..."

Her mother's voice faded abruptly and the whooshing and beeping grew so loud it made her clench her eyes shut. A shiver ran through her and suddenly she was choking, her mouth dry as sand and her body aching. Forcing her eyes open, she blinked and looked around at the hospital room, a hovering face taking her a minute to process.

"Connor?" she croaked, and he tipped a cup with some shaved ice against her lips.

"Here, take a little and let it melt. You're in the hospital, Em. You're going to be fine," Connor replied. The ice chips tasted like heaven as Emlen slowly swirled them around her mouth and swallowed the little bits of water they left behind. He offered another tip of the cup and she took it, trying to clear her mind of the haze and confusion.

"What happened?" she finally managed to whisper. Connor patted her shoulder gently. "There was a fire. Cullen got you out and I got the Rover out of the way. By the time I got back to you guys, someone had shot at you."

Em started to rise up at the word 'shot' but dropped back with a grunt of pain as she gasped out "Shot?" Her hand went to her side, feeling the thick bandages and the flare of pain as she touched it. "Who shot me?"

The nurse came in and shook her head. "You need to be resting, Miss Brewster. No moving around for a bit. Don't want to tear your stitches and staples now, do we?"

Connor sat beside her and took her hand while the nurse fussed and checked. "Cullen," she asked, voice cracking slightly.

"He's fine. Got a graze from a bullet, and they stitched him up. I left him sleeping in the waiting lounge. They told me you'd be waking so I wanted to be here for you," Connor replied, voice kept low.

"Don't worry about the shooter." His expression filled in the rest.

Emlen squeezed his hand, whispering "Thank you" as she lay back and closed her eyes again.

"Is the pain bad?" Connor asked. "No, just throbbing. My head still feels foggy and I keep trying to remember, but I'm only getting bits and pieces. Is the house gone?"

"Yeah. The fire department was hosing it down when we left, but the roof had caved in already."

Tears leaked down her cheeks and she hiccupped a sob before her hand lifted to cover her mouth.

"It's okay, Em. Let it out. You're alive. We're all alive." Connor leaned in and whispered in her ear, "I saved all the journals and your bag, and a few other things. Not much, but it's something."

Emlen reached up and slid her hand around his neck, pulling him in for a hug. "Thank you, Connor." Tears kept coming and she shook with the soft sobs, whimpering a little with the pain.

A cough at the door and Connor pulled back, taking her hands and resting them on the bed as he looked up at his brother. "Hey Cull. Feeling any better?"

The look on Cullen's face as he glared at his brother was there and gone, but Connor saw it and winced at what he knew would be coming.

Emlen smiled at Cullen and held out a hand. "You're okay."

Cull turned to Emlen and gave her a warm smile in return. "Yeah, I'm okay. Looks like you're going to be too."

She lifted a hand to him, and he moved closer, sitting on the edge of the bed as he took it. "I'm sorry about the house, Em."

A breath caught and she let it out, giving him a wry smile. "It's only things. We're all alive and that's really all that matters. That - and Connor saved the journals and my laptop. That would've set us back a lot."

"It would have, but like you said, we all made it out alive and that's what matters," Cullen replied before turning to Connor.

"Did you learn anything new?" Connor looked up from his phone and nodded. "Frankie was responsible for the fire and shooting you guys, but he's not bright enough to have been doing it on his own. He's working for someone and I'm trying to figure out who."

A memory tickled the back of Emlen's mind, and she closed her eyes, trying to grasp the thread that seemed to answer Connor's search...but it slipped away.

A huff of frustrated breath had Cullen squeezing her hand. "You hurting? Want me to call the nurse?"

"No," she grumbled. "I thought I remembered something but it's too hazy." Again, she pressed her fingers to the bandages. "How long am I going to be stuck in here?"

"Probably about a week. You had surgery, Em. The bullet didn't hit anything major, but it did tear through your body. Give yourself some time to heal, all right? Connor and I will take care of things for you. We can bring you anything you need to sign about the house and all of it. Just rest, okay?" Cullen held her hand between both of his for a moment, then shifted so his injured leg wasn't strained.

"What about your injury? You need to rest and heal too. In fact, go home and shower and sleep. Please. For me." Emlen's voice softened at the end and she tugged lightly on his hand to pull him close enough to brush a kiss. "Come back tomorrow, okay?"

Exhaustion had settled deep into his bones now that Cullen knew she would live. He kissed her back and started to rise, then nodded to Connor. "Hallway a moment?"

Connor sighed and nodded back, turning to Em. "I'll be back in a sec."

"No, you need to go home too," Em replied.

"I'll be right back," Connor repeated and stepped out into the hall behind Cullen, pulling the door shut behind him.

"I wasn't hitting on your girl, Cull. I was comforting my little sister, so get that thought right out of your head, all right?" Cullen opened his mouth, then snapped it shut and huffed. "Sure, didn't look innocent. But that's not the problem. You got Frankie, so that's good, but like you said, someone else is pulling the strings and I don't feel comfortable leaving her here with no one watching."

"I agree. She's still in danger. They've tried to kill her more than once, and they almost did it this time. I'll stay and see if I can get the captain to put guards on the room." Connor reached into his pocket and pulled out the keys. "My car is under the lights to the left of the door. Go get a shower and some sleep, huh? Oh...and the stuff is in my trunk. Maybe think about where to stash it - somewhere that's not your house?"

"Sounds like a plan. I'll see you in a few hours. And yes...I'll bring the coffee," Cullen replied and took the keys, heading for the elevator.

Connor watched him until he got on and then pulled out his phone, dialing. "Yeah, Captain. Sorry to wake you but my little sister was attacked tonight. The perp that did it is dead, but I don't think he was working alone. Can we get a detail put on her hospital room?"

18

Remembrance: Chapter Seventeen

It was close to seven in the morning by the time Connor had been able to leave Emlen in the care of a steady cycle of off duty plain clothes officers and the hospital staff. He'd got a ride home, showered, slept for a couple of hours and was now grabbing food to bring to Cullen. Pulling up to the house, he frowned when he didn't see Cullen's car outside. "He couldn't have gone out already, could he?" he muttered, phone ringing in his ear as he waited for his brother to answer. A groggy "'lo?" from Cullen had Connor relaxing as he asked, "Hey bro, where are you?"

The sound of squeaky springs and shifting fabric filled the phone before Cullen replied, "Uncle Joel's. Anything wrong?"

"No, just pulled up to your place and didn't see your car so wanted to find out where you were. I have breakfast. I'll be there in a few." Connor's gaze slid to where Emlen's house once stood. Smoke and ash lifted lightly in the morning breeze amid the ragged stone remains of the outer walls.

"Connor. Connor!" Cullen's voice snapped him out of his daze, and he shook himself. "Yeah, sorry, was thinking. What did you say?"

"I said, please bring lots of coffee and some juice, Cullen replied.

"Got it. On my way." Connor hung up and set the phone aside, pulling out of the driveway and heading to Joel's. That was probably the best place for Cullen to be right now. With Joel gone, no one would be looking for him there.

———◦———

Cullen hung the towel over the shower bar to dry and ran his fingers through his hair. An old Northeastern University t-shirt and a pair of sweats he'd left here at some point replaced the blood and soot-stained clothes he had been wearing. Grabbing the first aid kit, he headed out into the kitchen and put it on a counter, trying not to look at the spot on the floor where he'd found Joel's body. He'd called in a company to deep clean after the crime scene had been released and they had picked through the damage, throwing out anything that couldn't be salvaged and setting the stuff that could be in boxes that lined one wall of the living room. Then they'd cleaned the place, even scrubbing the bloodstain out of the tile floor and fixing the grout. No longer any visual evidence left that Joel's body had bled out in that spot, but Cullen could still see it every time he looked there. Taking a clean mug out of the cabinet, he filled it with water and tossed back a couple of headache tablets to take the edge off his pain. He didn't want to take the heavy-duty stuff the doctor had prescribed. Cullen needed his head clear to strategize with Connor.

Grabbing the kit and carrying his mug, he went to sit at the table and look out the window, waiting for Connor.

When Connor stepped into the house, Cullen could hear him pause and take in the changes - the missing furniture that had been smashed, the boxes neatly lined up, and the scent of pine disinfectant that filled the place instead of the scent of sweet tobacco and woodsmoke that they usually associated with Joel's place. He shut the door, spotting Cullen at the table and headed over, setting the cup holder down beside a couple of bags.

"You look a little better," he finally said, parceling out the food and pulling a jug of orange juice out and setting it down.

"Thanks for this," Cullen replied and picked up the juice, filling his used mug and downing it before starting in on the food and coffee. "I'm feeling better after sleep and a shower. Food should help too. Not much left in the kitchen after the cleaners were done."

"Captain got a few of the guys to do rotating shifts on Em's room for the next couple of days until we can get her out of there. Plain clothes, no uniforms, so as not to arouse interest." Connor swallowed the mouthful of breakfast sandwich and looked up at his brother. "We need to go over that stuff from Joel again. Maybe we can find something that tells us who is doing this."

"I'm betting on Jackson Junior," Cullen said, sipping his coffee and leaning back. "He's got to be the bio dad that Em was finding in her Mom's photos. That, coupled with the journals and then the photos from Joel's stuff..."

"Yeah, that's a good theory, but that's all it is. Theory. We will need incontrovertible proof to go after a potential vice president of the United States."

"We need proof for a lot of things. Like, did Frankie Kyle kill Joel? Who was he working for? Was it JJ or someone else? How many layers are there to this mess? We already know it goes back to before Emlen was born. Now, most of the primary sources from that time are dead or not about to talk to the two of us, even if one of us is still a cop." Cullen's fingers tapped the side of his cup as he sipped the coffee, feeling his brain start to churn faster as the caffeine hit.

"More basic than that, where is Em going to stay now that her house is gone?" Connor watched his brother, taking a swallow of his own coffee.

"I was going to say 'with me' at my place, but that's not safe. I think she should stay here with one of us with her," Cullen offered. "I have a feeling this place would be the last place someone would expect her to be with Joel dead. If he was alive, it would be different."

Something in his brother's voice had Connor narrowing his eyes. "What aren't you telling me?"

Cull put down his coffee and wiped his fingers on a napkin before leaning over and pressing a knot in the wood panel near his seat. It didn't look any different than any of the other pine knots showing through the stain on the walls, but this one made a soft 'click' and a door swung open. Reaching down into the space between the walls, he pulled out Emlen's messenger bag and lay it on the table before reaching in once more and taking out a box, setting it beside the bag. He glanced up at his brother and then opened the box, taking out the items inside. The wax sealed letter with his name on it, the velvet drawstring bag, the seal used on the wax, the silver handle tarnished with age, and last, an antique looking key.

"What is all this stuff?" Connor asked, reaching for the seal and turning it in his hands. It was about six inches long and about two inches in diameter and looked to be solid silver. The seal showed two knights on one horse, Templar crosses on their shields and a ring of words in Latin "Sigillum Militum." "Something...soldier," Connor muttered and pulled out his phone. A quick search and he said, "Sigillum Militum, seal of the soldier." His gaze lifted to his brother, expression confused but a glint of excitement lit his eyes.

Dumping the velvet bag's contents onto the table, Cullen saw a solid gold signet ring with the same design and words as the seal, and a pair of matching gold cufflinks. He shook his head then reached for the letter. "I've had this for a few days but haven't been able to bring myself to open it. I get the feeling that once I do, nothing will ever be the same again."

"Want me to open it?" Connor offered.

"No, I should. I just...." Cullen let out a slow breath. "... I've been having weird dreams and they all center around this symbol..." he pointed to the ring "...and this letter. I know it's something big, but I really don't want my life to change this much."

"Dreams? What kind of dreams? Why didn't you say something?" Connor leaned forward. "Cullen open the letter. Just because you read it doesn't mean you have to do anything."

He reached out to take the letter from the table and Cullen dropped his hand on it, pulling it back. "I'll do it." He turned the letter over and put a thumb on either side of the seal, snapping it open. Folding the pages back, he didn't see words for a moment, just the familiar scrawl of Joel's handwriting - the same scrawl he saw on birthday and holiday cards since he could remember. A slow breath in and Cullen started to read.

"Read it out loud, for chrissake." Connor snapped after a moment and Cullen snorted softly before starting at the beginning.

Cullen, If you're reading this, then I'm gone. I'm sorry I wasn't able to explain any of this to you in person. I hadn't realized the time had come to do so until after you and Emlen showed up to talk about her mother's murder case. I have known who ordered her mother murdered for years but have been unable to make any moves beyond that and I'll explain why. But first, some history. I know you know the history of the Knights Templar - at least the history that is commonly known in academia. However, the Vatican's history with the Templars is much different - and more recent. Over the last few centuries, members of the Order of the Knights Templar have infiltrated the church with the express goal of taking positions of power in the Vatican. They have also found seats on the boards of many major corporations and in the governments of several countries. Why? Access to resources. For example, the Vatican holds more rare documents and artifacts than any library or museum in the world. Anyway, the Order, as we refer to it, has several tasks it undertakes - one being the guarding of the line of Charlemagne from his second son, Charles the Younger.

History states that Charles died without children, but that is not the case. He and Aelfflaed did marry and had a daughter. Later, they had a son.

History doesn't know of this because the Druids made a deal with Charlemagne at the time and while the Chartres Cathedral was theirs and his - the children were theirs alone. When the eldest was about five, the children were taken by the Druids and trained. Both were blessed - or as some say - cursed - with powers that have continued down through their bloodline. Emlen's father is of that line, as is Emlen. Each member of the bloodline that has gifts is given a guardian, or a Garda. The Garda's job is to protect the Blood from any harm and help them explore their gifts. I was pregnant Camille's Garda. You, Cullen, are now Emlen's.

I failed her mother, and, in my shame, I failed her. I should have been there to guide her and protect her and instead I lost myself. Over the past three years, once I retired from the force, I had always been keeping a remote eye on her and making sure she had someone I trusted nearby. Rory Marks and Evan Ames are both good men who have acted as her security over the past three years. You can trust them. They will help get you up to speed.

Expect a call in a couple of weeks from Cardinal McKinsey. He's the Dean of the College of Cardinals for the Vatican - and His Eminence is the current head of the Order. I don't think I have to tell you to keep this all secret. Only you, Connor, and Emlen can share this information. I won't tell you to not tell Connor - you have never kept secrets from each other, and I don't expect you to start now.

Why are you getting this and not Connor? You're the one the Seer saw as Emlen's Garda. Connor is your Second - your backup and support in this task. Who was my Second? Your father. I know you have a lot of questions that I can no longer answer. Use the resources I have given you and you will find the answers. I love you both as if you were my own sons. Emlen is important - don't fail her like I did her mother. Always, Your Uncle, Joel DeSantis

Cullen sat back, the pages dropping to the table as he stared at his brother in silence.

"Holy shit," Connor whispered, staring back. He picked up the pages and shuffled them before finding the last page with names and contact information for the Cardinal and the two security men before setting it all back down on the table. "Magic? Seers? Fucking Knights Templar?"

Cullen finally spoke. "What the actual fuck did we just read?"

Pulling out his phone, Connor tapped it for a few moments then looked up at him. "The names all check out. I don't think this is some drunken rambling. I think it's true."

"Dad. We need to talk to Dad. If he knows about this, he can help. Right?" Connor nodded.

"Yeah, if we can convince him to talk about it. We'll have to show him the letter and the other stuff. He's supposed to be coming up for a couple of weeks with Mom at the end of the month. Maybe we can get them to come sooner."

"I think we need to talk to him today - and not say anything to Em until we know more. She's got enough on her plate right now," Cullen said, picking up the ring and cufflinks and putting them back in the bag, then putting everything else into the box once more. "I guess that explains the photo of Joel with Camille and little Emlen."

"Yeah, it does. Makes me wonder about all the photos of Joel with Em's grandfather, though. If the lineage is through her father's line, why was Joel friends with her mom's father?" Connor mused as he reached for his now cold coffee.

Cullen glanced at the time on his phone and turned to slide the box and the messenger bag back into the hiding spot and clicked the door shut. "I want to go see Emlen."

"Sounds good. I'll call the folks and see if I can get them to come up sooner. I'll use Joel's memorial service as a reason why."

"That's in a couple of weeks, right?" Cullen asked as he cleaned up the breakfast mess and made sure he had his wallet and keys.

"Two weeks. Hopefully we can get Em settled here before that. You find the boat keys so we can take the ashes out into the harbor?"

"That's the plan. I have the boat keys on my ring. Oh, and thank Tim again for driving my car here and bringing yours back. I barely remember him coming by I was so out of it last night."

"He's a good kid, but yeah, I got him a gift card for dinner at Moe's. He can take his girl out with it," Connor replied.

"Nice. Okay, call me when you find out what the folks are doing. I'm going to stop at the store and pick up a few things for Em, so she has something besides a hospital gown to wear. See you later," Cullen called over his shoulder as he locked up and Connor drove away.

Cullen glanced around the deck and the cove where Joel's boat was docked. It still felt weird to be here without Joel. Pulling his keys out, he got in his truck and drove away.

19

Remembrance: Chapter Eighteen

Emlen reclined in bed, reading on her phone when Cullen arrived, a duffel bag in one hand and a bag of food in the other. "Hey Emlen," he offered as he set the stuff down and leaned over to brush a kiss to her cheek, "How're you doing?"

"Bored out of my mind," Emlen replied, smiling up at him. "What's with all the stuff?" He reached for the bag and started to unpack it.

"Nurse said you were okay for solid food, so I got you your favorite muffins and coffee from the Main Street bakery."

"My hero." Em laughed and then winced, hand pressing to her side. "Ow, laughing hurts. Thank you." She peeled open the muffin and started eating as Cullen pulled the duffel bag up beside her.

"I picked you up a few things. I used the sizes of the clothes in your gym bag in your car. Figured you would feel better in something besides a hospital gown."

Setting the muffin down and opening the bag wider, she blinked a few times and then looked up at him. "You're amazing," Em whispered and then spent a few moments looking at everything. "Help me up, please. I want to brush my teeth and put on something else."

He got her into the bathroom and then waited to help her back onto the bed. She was walking on her own, but slow and stiff, and he smiled as he saw her come out in the lavender unicorn t-shirt nightgown and matching fuzzy socks. "Feel better?"

"Gods, yes. Much better, thank you." She pointed at the unicorn. "Really though?" Her grin showed she was teasing him. "I'm not exactly a virgin."

Cullen blushed as he tucked her back into the bed. "But you're a rare treasure, so it seemed appropriate."

Her heart stuttered a little at his words and she sighed inwardly, falling even more in love with the man every time he did something like this. "Doc says that I am doing well and can go home tomorrow as long as I come in twice a week for wound care. I did some checking around, there are cottages I can rent by the week on the other side of town."

Cullen shook his head as he sat down beside the bed and took her hand. "Connor and I had a better idea. I had thought about you staying with me, but it's too close to your place and too easy to find you there." His voice dropped low and he leaned in more. "We cleaned up Joel's place and think that would be best. You can be there and one of us can be with you, and make sure you're safe."

Emlen tipped her head, watching his face. "Even though the guy that shot us is dead, you still think I'm in danger?"

"Frankie Kyle, the guy that shot us, is not smart enough to have coordinated all of this. Someone else was pulling his strings. And we got a lot more information from a couple of letters Joel left behind that Connor is checking on before we share it. What do you say, you okay with staying at Joel's for a bit?"

"I guess so. It makes sense. So, what kind of information?"

Cullen laughed. "I knew that would be the first thing you wanted to know. Connor's calling our folks and seeing if they will come up earlier than they planned to attend Joel's memorial service, and we can all talk to them then. I'll tell you more later." He glanced around the room before adding, "When we have more privacy."

"You know that's gonna drive me crazy now, right?" Emlen gave him a wry smile, picking up her second muffin to take a bite of the blueberry treat.

Reaching for the second cup of coffee in the tray, Cullen leaned back, smirking. "That's the idea. Give you something else to obsess over." His smile faded a bit and he sipped his coffee, watching her eat. "The fire and police departments have both locked down the scene at your house. Arson investigators and police are all over it. It could be a week or more before we are allowed to go back there. My place is just too close, and they'd look there anyway. That's why we came up with Joel's. No one would consider it, with him gone and it still keeps you close enough to stay involved. I'm glad you're not fighting me on it. I don't want to fight, I just want you safe. Ideally, I'd love to ship you to Europe or something where no one would look, but I'm too selfish." He reached for one of her hands and rubbed his thumb over her knuckles. "I don't want to be that far away from you."

Emlen's lips curled into a faint smile. "I'd like to see Europe with you sometime, but you're right. Being in the area means we can keep investigating." She leaned back in the bed with her coffee, one hand still in Cullen's grasp.

Cullen sat there, torn between his need to protect her and his desire to tell her what they knew. Or what they didn't know but knew how to get the answers. Joel said he knew who it was that ordered the murder, but he didn't give them a name - just said the Cardinal would call him. Patience was not something he had a large supply of when it came to Emlen.

"You're awful quiet," Emlen said after a few moments. "What's going on?"

"Sorry, just lost in thought." Cullen smiled at her. "I brought you cotton drawstring pants and loose shirts so there wouldn't be pressure against your side. A couple of camisoles and sports bras and things like that."

"I saw. That was sweet of you. I'll pay you back when I get out of here."

"No, you don't have to pay me back. It wasn't much, just wanted you to be comfortable. Brought you a couple of books from those authors you like too."

"Much appreciated. There's only so many games of Candy Crush a person can stand." Em chuckled and set the coffee down, letting her head fall to the pillow and closing her eyes. "Stay with me for a little bit? I'm falling asleep, but it's so nice having you here."

"Of course, love. Sleep. I'll watch over you for a bit." Cullen leaned in and brushed a kiss to her lips before sitting back, still holding her hand. He watched as her breathing deepened and her body relaxed. He couldn't get over how quickly she'd woven herself into his life. Oh, there had been other women, other 'serious' relationships - even one he considered marrying once - but he wanted what his parents have had for the last forty-five years and Sheila wouldn't give him that, so he broke it off. His mom always told him that he'd find love when he stopped looking for it.

He'd have to tell her she was right. Lifting Emlen's hand, he pressed a kiss to her fingers before settling it down on the bed.

Leaning back, he picked up his coffee and absently sipped, rolling the bits of information around in his head. Still no call from His Eminence and he was getting antsy. Just then, his phone vibrated with an incoming call - it was Connor. "Hey, Connor."

"Hey, how's Em?"

"Sleeping again, but she's doing a lot better. They say she can leave tomorrow."

"Let's see if we can get her out tonight," Connor replied, his voice tight. "In fact, I'll make a few calls and you can bring her over tonight."

"What happened?" Cullen asked, sitting up. "Your house was broken into. Nothing taken that I can see, but all your papers were tossed, and your computer bag was shredded. Guess you hid the laptop?"

"Shit. Yeah, I did. It's in the fold-out couch."

"Nice. Okay, I'll be sure to get it and your spare ammo. I've packed you a bag already. I'll call you back soon," Connor replied.

"Thanks, brother. Appreciate it," Cullen said before they hung up. Running a hand through his hair, he rose and started cleaning up the room and packing up the bag they'd picked up for Emlen's stuff. Once he was done, he sat again and watched her sleep. If that Cardinal didn't call him in the next couple of days, he was going to try and track his number down himself.

20

Remembrance: Chapter Nineteen

It was late and the brothers sprawled in front of the empty fireplace, bottles of beer in hand. Emlen slept soundly in the back bedroom where they'd locked the storm shutters over the window. No one could get to her without a lot of noise or going through the two of them.

For the first time in a long time, Cullen breathed a little easier. "Thanks for doing whatever you did to get her released early. I really appreciate it. I can actually feel the stress easing a bit."

"Captain called, said the risk factors were increasing and if she was able to leave now instead of in twelve hours, it would be a personal favor. So, they let her go," Connor spoke, voice thick with exhaustion.

"Go get some sleep, brother. I slept off and on at the hospital, so I'll take first watch. I'll wake you in about four hours for my turn." Cull nodded at the stairs. "Go on. We need to stay alert."

"Good idea. See you in a few," Connor replied, not even arguing the point. He put the bottle down and stretched, stumbling a little towards the stairs.

Cullen listened until he heard the old iron bed frame creak with his brother's weight settling on it before he rose to walk to the front windows, peering out through the holes in the storm shutters. They had the house boarded up as if it were abandoned, their vehicles parked at a neighbor's place in the trees. The only thing he'd seen moving out there were ducks and seagulls, but he couldn't get rid of the feeling they were being watched. Tension curled along the back of his shoulders and he nearly jumped out of his skin when his phone vibrated.

Fumbling in his pocket, he tugged it free and glanced at the screen.

Unknown number. Lifting it to his ear, he tapped the button and spoke. "O'Brien here."

"Is the Descendant doing well?" a rich baritone rumbled into the phone, a faint accent in the words.

"The who?" Cullen asked. "Who is this?"

"Cardinal McKinsey, at your service. You can call me Liam, for now. Formalities are for events, not between those who will, I assume, be working together. May I call you Cullen?"

It took him a minute to process before Cullen let out a breath and nodded as he spoke. "Yes, you may call me Cullen, Your Eminence."

"Liam, please. Now, can you tell me if Emlen is doing well?"

"She's sleeping upon release from the hospital. We, my brother and I, have her secured somewhere safe and are taking care of her."

"At Garda Joel's cottage, yes, I know. I have dispatched a team to assist in protection detail."

"A what?" Cullen was surprised - and angry - yet, pleased that his feeling of being watched wasn't some result of exhaustion, paranoia or all of the above.

"Gee, good thing you called then. I'd hate to have shot someone, thinking they were an enemy." Sarcasm was thick in his tone.

"We've been a bit busy, getting things set up on our end, since Garda Joel was murdered. He had contacted me just days before, informing me that you were selected and that he would be beginning your training. I'm sorry that that did not happen. You did get his letter though, yes?" The Cardinal paused before continuing. "Of course you did, you wouldn't have known who I was if you did not. Trying to coordinate across the ocean is not as easy as it should be. Not when we have to be selective about whom we trust with certain information."

Anger shivered through Cullen and he knew the Cardinal could hear it in his voice. "And we've been a bit busy here, trying to stay a step ahead of someone who clearly wants Emlen dead. We almost died the other night, and the three of us would have if my brother wasn't so skilled. So, pardon me if I don't think a fucking phone call is too much to expect." Yeah, he probably shouldn't be swearing to a priest, but he really couldn't care less about that right now.

"I'm sorry, my son, that we weren't aware of things sooner," the Cardinal replied, voice even and calm. "Both you and Connor have done amazingly well with the situation, but it's time we sat down and had a discussion."

"And that's a great idea, except I'm not leaving Emlen and she's in no condition to travel."

"Well, then. I guess it is providence that I will be docking near your hideout in the next thirty minutes. Don't wake the girl, but it would be useful to have your brother included in the conversation. I'll see you shortly."

The call disconnected before Cullen could get another word out. It took every ounce of his self-control to keep from throwing the phone into the fireplace. A stifled sound of frustration blew past his lips and he turned to head up the stairs, stopping on the bottom step. Connor had only had a little over an hour's sleep and this putz wasn't about to show up in the next ten minutes, so Cullen decided to let Connor sleep until someone showed up. Retracing his steps, he headed into the kitchen to make a pot of coffee. He needed all of his senses on alert for this conversation.

21

Remembrance: Chapter Twenty

Liam, Cullen, Connor, and three of the Cardinal's escorts stood in the screen porch off to the side of Joel's house. It was shielded by huge lilac bushes and the door to the inside left open so they could hear if Emlen called out. One of the escorts pulled cushions out of a storage bench and lay them on the chairs while they all held coffee mugs, waiting for the all clear from the group doing a circuit of the property to make sure they were safe - and alone.

Cullen stared at the Cardinal, taking in his pressed black slacks, polished combat boots and buttoned polo shirt beneath a light, black zip-front jacket. He was a fit man who carried himself with military precision. White hair in a crew cut, clean shaven, and bright blue eyes in a tanned face that showed the lines of a life spent carrying burdens not his own. Cullen guessed the man to be in his early sixties, but he moved like a man half his age.

When the all clear came back, the Cardinal sat and gestured to the brothers to sit as well. The other three stood around the space, eyes watchful, ears tuned to the chatter in an earbud tucked discreetly in place. "Thank you for taking the time to speak with me," he began but Cullen raised a hand to stop him.

"First, let's get something straight. This is our place. Joel left it to us. As a guest in our home, I expect you to be considerate and follow the rules." Cullen fully expected him to behave, but it was always best to lay the cards on the table in a situation like this. His parents taught him the rules of hospitality, but Joel had instilled the strategic benefits such rules brought into play.

"I see Joel did train you, even if he didn't explain what he was training you for," the Cardinal replied.

"Actually, our parents taught us the rules of hospitality," Connor spoke up. "Joel just taught us the strategic benefits of those rules." He took a swallow of his coffee and leaned back, eyes glittering in the dim light through the bushes as he watched the man across from him.

"Well, I'm no Sidhe, but I give you my word and my bond that I will honor those rules," the Cardinal said, a faint smile playing around his lips.

Cullen leaned in, elbows on the arms of the chair, cup cradled in his hands, his gaze locked on the man's eyes as he spoke. "So, Liam, why are you here and what is it with calling Emlen 'the Descendant'?"

"Right to the point, I see. Well, I need to give you a little background. What do you know of Charlemagne?"

Cullen answered, "Charles the Great, king of the Franks in the late seven hundreds to early eight hundreds and emperor of the west. He founded the Holy Roman Empire and brought about a cultural revival. The Carolingian Renaissance, I believe it was called."

"Yes, exactly. And while he did found the Holy Roman Empire, he was not wholly against other religions. He was a particular patron of the Cathedral of Chartres in France and there is a massive stained-glass window that is called the Charlemagne window." He took a sip of his coffee, then continued. "The cathedral is lovely and a historical treasure, but that's not why it is important. It was built on a leyline that links Glastonbury, Stonehenge and the Pyramids of Egypt.

"Before Christianity, it was a sacred site for a sect of druids known as the Carnutes. Legend has it that the druids believed it to be a place where spiritual energy emanated from beneath the earth in a spring or well that increased fertility and blessings on those who would partake of the waters. Charlemagne made a pact with the druids and they blessed him with power, success, and glory. More specifically, they later blessed his son Charles the Younger.

"History says that Charles never married but had been betrothed to Aelfflaed and that he never had children. That is not the truth. Charles and Aelfflaed wed at Chartres when she was carrying their child. The druids gave the child the gift of magic."

"Wait...what?" Connor made a derisive noise and shook his head. "Come on, seriously? You're going to tell us a story about magic?"

Cullen held up a hand to his brother. "Wait, Connor. There are things we've both experienced that defied explanation. I mean, even Emlen's had some weird ghost-type experiences. We're Celts, we understand that some stuff just can't be explained." He looked at Liam. "However, just because we can't explain it, doesn't mean it's magic."

"Emlen's had experiences with ghosts?" Liam asked, voice rising in excitement as he leaned forward. "Then she's Awakening. This is great news."

Connor thudded back into his seat with a sigh of frustration. "I give up. The crazy train has left the station..."

Cullen let out a slow breath. "So, Emlen is a descendant of Charlemagne's grandchild. That's why you call her Descendant, right?"

"Precisely," Liam replied.

"But there must be tens of thousands of descendants by now. What makes Emlen so important?" Cullen continued. "If magic, or whatever, is in all of the descendants, why her?"

"It wasn't all of the descendants, just those who descended from Charles the Younger's child. They only had one, a daughter, and Edyth had four children, two sons and two daughters. One daughter had two children and died in childbirth, the other three children died before they had offspring. For some reason, it is rare for more than one child of a Descendant to actually have viable offspring." Liam spoke, his voice calm. "In Emlen's case, she is the only child born to the last living Descendant."

"So, someone might have ten kids but only one will have magical living offspring?" Connor asked, a tinge of horror in his words.

"Exactly. Either their children die young, they are unable to have children at all, or they die before reaching adulthood. Emlen is the only child of John Frederick Jackson, he himself the only surviving child of Simone Jackson, nee Valencia."

"If she's the last one, is that why someone is trying to kill her?" Cullen asked.

Liam hesitated and then replied, "I don't know. We don't know of any person or organization that currently wants the Descendants dead. Our job, as Garda, is to protect them from any type of attacks or risks. There have been organizations, usually tied to the church, that wanted to eradicate magic, but there isn't anything on our radar at this point in time."

"It's her father then, right?" Connor spoke for the first time in a few minutes.

"Not that we can tell," Liam said. "None of his communications or actions have led us to believe he is behind it."

"Then who?" Cullen asked. "We know Frankie was working for someone and he's dead after the last attempt. Do you have any way of figuring out who was pulling his strings?"

"We're working on it," Liam replied. "There were calls on his phone records that trace to Boston, Massachusetts, but it went to a burner phone and we haven't figured out who has it yet."

"Yet. Not even the NSA can figure out who is holding a burner phone unless they triangulate a call and get a CCTV to spot the person talking on it." Connor leaned forward, elbows on his knees.

"We have a few suspects and there are people watching them. If we can narrow it down—" Liam started but Connor interrupted.

"You have the kinds of resources for that level of surveillance?"

Liam gave him a faint half-smile and folded his hands across his stomach. "Yes."

Cullen leaned towards his brother and grinned. "Vatican, remember?"

Rolling his eyes at Cullen, Connor looked back at the Cardinal. "Emlen able to know about all of this? Some of this? None of this? How does this all..." a hand waved in the air "...work?"

"Often, the Descendants don't know details. For example, Joel guarded Camille, Emlen's mom, because she was pregnant and then raising Emlen. It was imperative that Camille be protected in order for Emlen to thrive. When Camille was murdered, the focus, of course, shifted to the child. That's where, for a time, your father stepped in. That was terminated when Camille's family re-claimed the child and sent her to boarding school. For a few years, one of her teachers was her Garda, then we slipped two into her security detail when that was implemented." Liam chuckled a little. "She didn't make it easy, that's for sure.

At least, now, she's back where the two of you can step up and take over." His smile faded and he let out a breath, looking around the porch before back to the brothers. "Joel was taken from us much too soon. He would have been an excellent teacher and guide into the organization."

"Well, here's a stupid question." Cullen could feel the anger rising as he took in all the information. "If Emlen is one of two surviving Descendants, and you have this vast organization designed to keep them safe, how the actual fuck did anyone get even close enough to her to attempt murder more than once?"

Liam shook his head and let out a sigh. "It doesn't work like that. Yes, we have a lot of resources we can tap, but Garda are not on duty all the time. Like your father, he had been called up when assigned Emlen as a child and then released when she had been removed from his care. Her teacher watched her until she went to a different school and gained bodyguards. Your father still did his carpentry job, her teacher still does his teaching job, but for a period of time, they also did this. Make sense?"

Connor shrugged. "I get how the 'on duty, off duty' thing works, but what Cullen asked still holds. How did anyone even get close enough to her if you have all these people you can tap to watch her?"

"Free will and a reasonable expectation of privacy," Liam replied. "That, and we were still scrambling after Emlen's disappearance from Boston, no idea where she'd settled until Joel let us know she was here, and then the loss of Joel. We got here as soon as we could and hoped that Joel had explained enough to you so you could fill the gap until we could explain more."

"Well, what now?" Cullen asked, setting his cup aside.

"You give me your oath that you'll guard the Descendant. We make sure you have all the resources and contact information, and you continue doing what you've been doing. For our part, we will keep trying to track down whomever was pulling Frankie's strings, find the person behind the attacks, and deal with them," Liam replied.

"Let's get started," Connor said as he and Cullen nodded, then focused when Liam started to speak.

22

Remembrance: Chapter Twenty-One

Emlen put the cup down on the little table beside her, stretching carefully as she enjoyed the glimpses of the harbor between the lilac bushes. Ideally, she wanted to be out on the front deck, but the guys were still so paranoid about her safety. Right now, the screen porch presented a better option to get some alone time. There hadn't been much of it the last couple of weeks. Between Cullen, Connor, and the guards from the Cardinal, there was always someone around. It took almost three days of convincing before Cullen agreed to let her favorite hairdresser, Lacy Ann come do her hair and makeup for the event tonight. That was something else new.

In her research, she learned everything she could about her father and what he'd been up to the past twenty years. He had recently married his third wife, Elise Matthews and now stepping up his career in government from Senator of Massachusetts to Vice President to the highest office in the United States. Tonight's event, a fundraising gala for the campaign where the candidate for Vice President was the guest of honor. Hugh Bannerman, the candidate for President, would be at a gala in his hometown of Philadelphia, so the Boston event was all about John Frederick "JJ" Jackson. Dad.

A shiver ran through her, a mix of excitement and wariness at the thought of finally meeting him face to face at an age when she would remember him. Photos had told her that she had his hair color and eyes, definitely his eyes, as well as his height, but the rest she got from her mom. It was almost eerie how much she looked like him and she wondered if the similarities would be as striking in person. She hoped so. Emlen really hoped the shock of him seeing her in front of him would rattle him enough to say something he normally would not. A proven tactic she used as a reporter now and then, but this wasn't just some story, this was her life.

The brothers were not pleased with this plan and had argued against her attending at all. The Cardinal pulled rank and told them her plan had merit and they needed to fall in line or step back. He had then obtained tickets for Emlen and the brothers, who would go as her escorts.

They both had tuxes and she had a violet-hued silk Vera Wang that covered her scars and was still comfortable and elegant. Amber ear drops and her mother's pendant were all she planned to wear for jewelry. Never without the pendant, it became something her grandmother had often commented, insisting that it wasn't a fine gemstone. Her argument that she didn't need to wear it and have it ruin the look of an outfit never won. For some reason, Emlen just didn't feel comfortable without it. If she wasn't wearing it around her neck, it was tucked into her bra or wrapped around a wrist as a bracelet. Her fingers went to it now as her thumb rubbed the stone and she gave a crooked smile. She wondered if her father would recognize it or not. Well, tonight, she'd find out.

By the time the three were ready to go, Lacy Ann had left after doing Em's hair and makeup, hiding the last traces of bruising with her artful brushes and tugging her locks into a cascade of curls pulled up in front and cascading around her shoulders.

The three settled into the limo provided, again, by the Cardinal and Emlen accepted a sparkling water, not daring alcohol's dulling effects on a night like this. "I wish you guys could tell me more about what the Cardinal told you. I get that you don't want to worry me, but not knowing is worse."

"We swore an oath, Em," Connor answered, gaze shifting to his brother where he sat beside her while Connor sat facing them, back to the driver. "There's nothing we haven't told you that truly impacts you in any way."

Cullen looked away as his brother flat out lied to her and curled his fingers around her hand. "Just focus on tonight, love, and let us do our job of supporting and keeping an eye on you, all right?" He lifted her hand and kissed her fingers. "You're absolutely breathtaking, have I told you that yet?" A smile curled his lips as she rolled her eyes and sipped her drink before settling back into the rich leather seats.

"You did, but you can say it a few more times if you like," Emlen teased and looked from Cullen to Connor. "I've got the two most handsome escorts possible. I'm going to make so many women jealous."

They all laughed at that and reached to touch glasses in a toast.

"I know you're nervous, Em, but you don't look it," Cullen murmured. "You're going to be fine. If it turns out he doesn't want to know you, then it is his loss."

"And we'll make sure you're safe," Connor added. "Between us and the Garda set up in the hall, no one will be able to blink without someone watching." He sounded a little awed by the sheer number of resources the Cardinal had put into play for tonight. Of course, he and Cullen knew the reason was because the last two Descendants would be in one place.

The limo pulled up in front of the Boston Park Plaza hotel, a liveried footman opening their door and helping them out.

Emlen gripped her silver clutch until her knuckles were white, staring up at the entrance as the brothers each offered her an arm. Looping a hand through both, she headed inside, a breath catching as the sheer number of people swam before her. It had been a while since she had stepped into a crowd and after the attempts on her life, her desire to find a wall and flatten her back against it was overwhelming. Instead, she took a slow breath, pasted a smile on her lips and stepped into the room. A pair of guards stood by the door, checking identification as each person passed through, the coiled earbuds tucked into their collars made it likely they were Secret Service.

Just past them, a woman in a blue silk suit and white blouse checked their names and gave them their table assignments, chatting cheerily with many of the guests. "Emlen Brewster! Oh, my dear. I'm so sorry for your loss. Your grandmother was such a force of nature. Her absence will be felt by so many of us." The woman clutched Emlen's hand as she gushed at her and Em's look of confusion must have baffled her as much as her words had Em at a loss. Emlen stuttered, "I'm sorry, I don't know..."

Cullen wrapped an arm around Emlen and gave the woman a polite smile as he guided Em away. "Connor's looking it up. Keep smiling and I'll get you to the table."

Em let him guide her, her face feeling numb from smiling as her thoughts whirled. Her grandmother was dead? No one had even contacted her or...well, not like they could find her. She'd pretty much dropped off the map after the house fire. In the hospital, hidden away - of course they couldn't have told her. Her shoulders relaxed a little and she curled her fingers around Cullen's arm. "I'm all right," she murmured. "It was just a bit of a shock. It's not like I actually had any affection for the woman. She was never even remotely kind or loving towards me."

Connor joined them at the table and showed Emlen his phone with a police file pulled up on the screen. "They're calling it a botched home invasion attempt. She was shot the same day of your house fire."

Emlen's hand shook as she reached for the glass of water in front of her and took a careful sip. Somehow, the person who had been trying to kill her had also killed her grandmother. She had no proof, but her gut was telling her that it was all connected. "Maybe this was a bad idea, coming here."

"No, Em. It's time to face him and see if he's behind all of this. His reaction to seeing you will tell us everything, Cullen replied, taking her hand in his.

"You can do this." Connor added, a hand on her opposite shoulder, "We can do this. You're not alone. We're right here beside you."

A moment passed, then another before Emlen lifted her gaze. First looking at Cullen, then at Connor, she gave them both a smile. "Thank you, both of you. You're right, I couldn't do this alone, but with you guys, I can."

Cullen kissed her cheek and Connor squeezed her shoulder before they were interrupted by a man stepping up to the podium on the stage. Voices rose for a moment, then stilled as he leaned into the microphone. "I'm Brett Sellers, Mr. Jackson's chief of staff, and I want to welcome you all to our event this evening. In just a few minutes, Mr. Jackson will be taking the stage. Could I ask everyone to please find their tables and take their seats? Thank you."

Noise filled the room once more as people began milling about, finding their seats and greeting their table companions. Each table had been set for twelve, but only three other couples settled at their table, all offering polite greetings. Just when it looked like there would be some empty seats, another woman and two men sat near Connor and he nodded at them in greeting. Emlen recognized them as three of the Cardinal's protector team, dressed for the evening in tuxes - even the female member wore a woman's tux with a glittering sequined top underneath.

Em's hands were sweating and she reached for the linen napkin, scrubbing it between her palms under the table as she took slow breaths, doing her best to calm her nerves. She was about to see her father, in person, for the first time that she could remember. If she could, she would have wished for her mother's spirit to be there to comfort her, but she'd not heard or scented a trace of her since the house fire. A part of her worried that with the house gone, whatever held her mother's spirit here might have been destroyed. Her thoughts were interrupted by Sellers again at the microphone, then a growing roar of applause and "Hail Columbia" being played from the speakers.

Everyone got to their feet and Em rose as well, eyes on the curtain in back as it fluttered and then parted for John Frederick Jackson to step out onto the stage. Their table placed in the second row from the stage, a little off to the side so she had a very clear view of the man to whom she owed half of her biological makeup. Her breath caught for a moment and Cullen wrapped an arm around her waist, supporting her quietly. She gave him a quick, faint smile and turned back to see JJ trying to quiet the crowd as people re-took their seats. As people settled, her gaze was drawn to a man about her height, short white hair and a neatly trimmed moustache and goatee. A surge of memories from when she called him 'uncle' washed over her, colored now with the knowledge that he was much more than that. Time to challenge his watchful attention, his habitual sneer of disapproval; she rose to her feet and pulled away from Cullen, heading past the few tables that stood between them.

The Judge sat at the table front and center, about twenty feet from the stage where the floor had been cleared for the press photographers. Pride welled up in him as he watched his son take the podium, the roar of the crowd as much for him as it was for his son. He knew it was by his hand JJ was where he was now, and it was almost as heady a feeling as if he were up there himself. Oh, the boy had been distancing himself a bit from his dad as the race came to a close. Some of it had to do with that new wife of his, Elise. She didn't like the Judge and made sure JJ knew that being around his old man was not something she would participate in. He would just give it time. She'd get bored, they'd get divorced, like the other two, and a nice settlement would send her off to a very comfortable life as another Jackson divorcee. He had to tolerate her for now because the public preferred their leaders to be married, solid family men. Nothing was going to keep his son out of the Vice President's mansion, nor eventually out of the White House. Too bad his own late wife's selfish act of betrayal kept her from seeing this. John Cameron Jackson let himself savor the moment, eyes locked on his son's face, ears filled with the roar of the crowd until the moment was interrupted by a soft, female voice whispering in his ear.

"Hello, Uncle JC. Or should I say, Grandfather?" Emlen sat in the empty seat beside him and smiled. "It's been a while, hasn't it, Judge?"

He stared at her in disbelief for a moment, then fury surged, turning his pale face red. "How dare you show up here tonight? You stupid girl, do you have any idea the damage you could do to JJ's campaign?"

Em laughed at that, a bright, loud sound that rang out over the nearly quiet room, drawing attention from everyone nearby - including her father at the podium. She turned to look at him and with one look at the expression on his face, she felt in her heart he didn't have anything to do with the murders or attempts. He looked stunned, happy, and awed as he turned to make his way along the stage to the stairs. Emlen shifted her gaze back to the Judge. Deciding to follow her gut, she let out a soft breath. "It was all you, wasn't it? My Mom, Joel, the attempts on me. It was all your doing."

The Judge couldn't seem to speak, his face flushing dark red. Bolting to his feet, he grabbed her arm and jerked her out of the chair, turning and slamming into Cullen's chest. Connor stood to the other side, blocking an easy exit. Emlen reached for the hand gripping her arm and grabbed one of his fingers, bending it backwards until he released her.

Just then, JJ approached the group. Having seen his father grab Em, he glared at the old man and turned to her. "Are you okay? You're Emlen, right?" As she nodded, he held out a hand to her, his eyes shining wetly, voice cracking. "Gods, you look just like your mother."

"She looks just like you." Elise said from beside him, a warm smile on her face. "Hello, Emlen. I've heard so much about you."

The crowd muttered and stared while Sellers got to the podium. "A temporary delay, everyone. Everything's fine, please enjoy the drinks and appetizers the staff are bringing around, and we'll be back on program shortly."

Music drifted from the speakers set around the room, but the group front and center didn't even notice.

Emlen put her hand in her father's and moved towards him just as the Judge grabbed both of their wrists and tore them apart, practically panting as he snarled at them.

"What the fuck do you two think you're doing?"

"Enough, Father," JJ hissed at him and jerked his arm away as a Secret Service agent stepped up to the table, eyes on the old man.

Emlen, however, had had enough, and she grabbed her grandfather's wrist in return, sinking her fingernails into his skin. "Keep your hands off of me," she snarled and stepped closer to JJ once she was free.

Elise came up on her other side and put an arm around her, glaring at the Judge, and said, "Still trying to intimidate women, eh Judge? Pathetic!"

Cullen and Connor moved to hem in the Judge a bit more and keep him from grabbing anyone else as JJ turned to Em.

"May I hug you?" he asked, voice still choked with emotion.

Emlen just nodded and stepped into his embrace, breathing in the scent of him. Memories of no real substance rose as she took a breath of remembered after shave and cigar and she smiled, glancing up at him. "I remember that smell," She whispered. "We have a lot to talk about."

"Yes, we do," JJ replied and glanced at Elise. "Isn't she beautiful?"

"Yes, she is." Elise smiled at him and put a hand on Emlen's shoulder. "But you, my love, have a speech to give. I'm sure Emlen and her escorts would be happy to wait a few minutes for you to get that done so we can spend some time getting to know each other?"

Emlen nodded and glanced over at Cullen and Connor, both smiling at her. Cullen nodded back and Connor gave her a thumbs up before she turned to the couple and let out a breath. "We'd be honored. Thank you."

A frustrated, furious roar spilled from the Judge's lips as he pulled a gun from behind his back and pointed it at the trio. "NOOOO!" he shouted as Connor grabbed for his gun, shoving the arm upwards as it went off. Cullen then tackled the Judge before the Secret Service could even get around the table, taking all three of them to the floor.

Chaos exploded in the room, people screaming and racing for the exits or diving under tables while JJ was bodily grabbed and forced away. His shouts for Elise and Emlen caused the other agents to grab the women and hustle them behind JJ.

Em tried to see what was happening to the brothers, but she got lifted right off her feet and carried by the two agents holding her. She barely got her feet under her before all three were put into a black SUV and rushed from the hotel. Shaking and breathing fast, the three of them looked around before Emlen grabbed for her phone in her clutch. Her hands shook so, she could barely get the number hit and held the phone to her ear. "Voicemail," she whispered and looked up at JJ and Elise across from her. "What the hell was all that?"

JJ was holding Elise close, one hand resting splayed across her belly as he looked up at Em. "My father and your grandmother were responsible for splitting up Camille and I, and for keeping me from being with you. When Camille got killed, I tried to get custody, but your family refused. My father had my name erased from your birth certificate and any record of me with your mother got buried. We had been engaged when you were born, but I wasn't as strong a person then and I let their threats separate us. For that, I am sorry."

Elise patted his arm lightly, leaning forward as the vehicle rocked back and forth before racing into a parking garage and down several levels. She then continued the story. "The Judge never allowed anyone to speak about you or your mother. When JJ and I talked about marriage, he sat down and told me everything. To be blunt, we were hoping the old man would die soon and we could finally reach out to you."

It was a lot to take in and Emlen's mind raced. "My grandmother is dead. I just found out tonight." She wet her lips and looked out the window as the agents checked the surroundings before opening the doors and ushering them all out and into an elevator. "Where is this?" she asked.

"Our city penthouse. Where we stay when JJ's working in town. Mostly where we are unless it's a weekend and we can get away for a couple of days," Elise replied, stepping into the suite and kicking off her shoes. "Come on in and I'll get us something to drink. Tea sound good?"

Emlen nodded, looking at the stunning view of the city through a wall of windows, the colors and furnishings evoking a warmth and feeling of home she hadn't expected from a penthouse suite. Sitting on a plush chair, she looked down at her phone again and texted Cullen to call her as soon as he could, letting him know that she was fine.

JJ came in a moment later, shutting the door and leaving the agents outside before tugging his tie loose. "Well, Emlen, this is not how I planned our reunion going." He gave a wry chuckle as he sat across from her. He leaned forward, elbows on his knees, hands clasped. "So, the O'Brien brothers, huh? Good choice as your Garda."

Em's mouth dropped open, then closed with a snap. "Right, of course you know about this. I just learned about it a couple of weeks ago. I still know very little. Apparently, the Cardinal thinks it's too much for me to handle all at once." Her tone full of sarcasm and frustration.

"Well, McKinsey can be a real pain in the ass, but he's good people nonetheless." JJ replied and accepted a mug of tea from Elise before she put down another in front of Em. "One sec," she murmured and soon returned with a tray with milk and sugar, lemon wedges and a plate of chocolate chunk cookies.

Wrapping her hands around the mug, Em took a sip and offered a soft 'thanks' to Elise before her gaze went back to her father. "Why did the Judge kill my mother? Joel? Why did he try and have me killed more than once?"

Setting his mug down, JJ reached for Elise's free hand as she settled next to him on the sofa, tucking her feet up under her and sipping her own tea. "It started when my sister died. We knew about the powers from the time we were kids. Tina was a couple of years older than I, and she was telekinetic." His expression softened when he spoke of her. "She went to Europe for a gap year before starting college. We still don't know what happened to her, but my mother knew without a doubt that she had died. The power lineage is through my mother's line and when Tina died, the power went to the eldest living Descendant - my mother." He reached for his tea and sipped before speaking again, staring into the mug. "The knowledge of Tina's death and the lack of any body or evidence of her dying drove my mother to suicide. When she killed herself, all of her power came to me." His gaze lifted to Emlen's face. "The only thing I can think of is that my father wanted your power to come to me, too, to help cement the election."

Emlen's face showed her confusion for a moment as she processed what he said and then her gaze lifted to his. "So, my mother wasn't the target that night. I was." She closed her eyes and let out a breath before looking at the couple across from her. "He's not going to stop."

"Well, after tonight, I can stop him," JJ replied. "He pulled a gun and attempted murder. I will have him declared insane and institutionalized. He has stage three prostate cancer. The chances of him surviving it are slim, so we'll just lock him away until he's gone." There was no emotion, no sense of loss in his tone as Emlen listened to his words. A shiver ran through her and she cupped the mug a little closer for warmth. A buzz from her phone had Emlen reaching for it, setting the mug down as she read the text.

"Cullen and Connor are on their way. The Judge has been taken to Mass General for a psych hold and is under guard." Weariness washed over her and Em pushed to her feet. "If it's fine with you, I'd like to go home and talk more tomorrow?"

"Of course, Emlen," JJ said, rising. "I'll let the agents know to escort you downstairs." He pulled a business card from his jacket and handed it to her. "My private cell is on there. Call me tomorrow, and we'll talk more, okay?"

Em took the card and slid it into her clutch, then turned to Elise. "I'm glad you're okay." She paused, dizziness washing over her, enough to have her dropping back to the chair. "I'm... I don't feel so good."

"That's the drugs taking effect. You'll be out soon. Don't worry, we'll let the brothers know you decided to stay overnight." Elise said, reaching for Em's phone as it started to slip from her hands.

JJ lifted her from the chair and cradled her close. "We've got a lot of catching up to do. Can't let you leave just yet daughter."

The darkness wrapped around her and Emlen heard no more.

23

Remembrance: Chapter Twenty-Two

Emlen stirred, waking slowly. Her mouth dry as dust and her head throbbed in time with her heartbeat. The room was blessedly dim as she peeled her eyes open and carefully looked around. It wasn't a room she recognized, as charming and comfortable as it appeared. A wrought iron bed with a bright quilt that had been tucked around her, an old rocking chair, a dresser, and a pair of side tables. Sitting up, she swung her feet over the side of the bed and felt the room sway before it settled once more. Glancing down at herself, she saw she was in her silk slip and underwear and it took her a lot longer than it should have to process that her violet gown lay over a bench at the foot of the bed, her shoes set neatly beside.

Between one breath and the next, the events of the evening came flooding back to her and she eyed the glass of water on the bedside table with distrust. Rising, she headed towards the gleam of porcelain that hinted at an en suite bath and ran the cold tap, using her hands to cup water to her mouth. Rinsing her face and brushing strands of hair out of the way, she examined her reflection and decided the smudged and smeared makeup had to go.

Scrubbing her face and giving herself a quick wash made her feel more alert. She finished up using the facilities before going back to pick up her dress. Beneath it lay some folded clothes and she shook them out, figuring the yoga pants and t-shirt probably belonged to Elise. Tugging off the slip, she pulled on the borrowed clothes and rolled everything up in her gown. A pair of stretch sneakers were under the bench and she put them on, the fit a little loose but better than barefoot or heels. She didn't see her clutch or phone anywhere, so decided to get out of the room and try her luck. Stepping out into the hallway, she paused and listened. Em could hear raised voices in the main room and smelled food cooking, so she took a breath, squared her shoulders and moved forward. Her father sat at a table in front of the floor to ceiling windows with Elise. Beyond them, the Boston skyline shimmered in the afternoon sun.

"I don't suppose you've seen my purse and phone anywhere, have you?" she asked as she moved towards them. "I really need to get going. I've a job to get back to."

They both looked up at her and JJ rose, a polite smile on his face. "We've got too much to talk about, daughter. Your belongings will be returned before you leave. For now, sit and Elise will get you a plate."

Elise rose, glaring at him before heading towards the open plan kitchen and picking up a plate and some silverware, dropping it noisily on the table at an empty chair.

Emlen folded her arms around the bundle of clothing in her arms and shook her head. "I'm not hungry. I want my things and then I'll go. You can call and we can talk another time. Unless you're holding me prisoner here, the game is over."

"Holding you prisoner?" JJ laughed, shaking his head. "You had too much to drink and we put you up in the guest room. How is that holding you prisoner?" Elise remained silent, glaring at JJ the whole time. Apparently, she'd interrupted a quarrel of some kind, but Emlen didn't care. She just wanted to get out of there. 'Drank too much, my ass' ran through her thoughts as she glared at him.

"Good, then I'll be going now. My purse, please?" Emlen held out her hand and just waited. After what felt like five minutes, but was probably closer to one, Elise rose and pulled her purse out of a cabinet under the wine rack, handing it to Em before retaking her seat. Emlen opened it, saw her phone and turned towards the door, lips clamped tight. She didn't dare speak because once she got started, she knew she'd end up shouting more than conversing.

Em pulled the door open, gave a nod to the two Secret Service agents outside, and just before the door closed, she heard JJ speak, shutting the door before he was finished. All she heard was "You'll be hearing..." and then the thud of the door behind her. Her feet didn't slow until she was in the elevator, fidgeting as it descended. She speed-walked out of the building and onto the sidewalk. Once outside, she took a deep breath and felt the trembling start. Fingers fumbled with her phone as she called Cullen. "Come get me, please. I'm outside Garden Towers and I need a ride."

"I'm on my way. There's a coffee shop a couple of doors down. Go there and wait. I'll tell Connor, he's back at home. I'm about twenty minutes away," Cullen replied.

They kept the conversation to a minimum and no details, something they'd drilled into Em over the past couple of weeks. You never knew who was listening. Sitting in the coffee shop, back against the wall, bundle of clothes tucked beside her, Emlen wrapped her fingers around the cup and sipped, eyes on the windows that bordered two sides of the shop.

She relaxed a touch when she recognized two of the Cardinal's guards take seats near the door, keeping an eye on her and the traffic around them. She'd come to recognize the usual crew after the past few weeks of seeing them around the cottage and the grounds. Sitting with her coffee gave her time to process and realize that it had been only a month since she'd nearly been killed, since her house burned down, and she and Cullen had been shot. Three weeks since she'd learned about the Garda and the fact she was one of two living Descendants of Charlemagne's magical lineage.

Em knew there was a lot more she hadn't been told, but to be honest, she'd heard enough at the time. It was a lot to process, the idea that she had some kind of magical gift and that she was one of a long line stretching back nearly fifty generations. The only things she could do that she saw as different from normal people was talk to her mother's ghost and have a good instinct if someone was telling her the truth or not. Even those could be chalked up to mental instability and a solid gut if one were being realistic. Em sipped her coffee and looked at the glittering purse on the table beside her. The night before had been full of anticipation and fear. She rubbed two fingers between her brows, soothing the lines furrowed there as she tried to put all the pieces together.

The judge and her grandmother were connected somehow. Her grandmother, as she'd learned last night, had died in some kind of home invasion. That stank to high heaven, because she knew her grandmother wasn't liable to open her own door, nevermind to someone she didn't know. She also had security measures in place at home, being that she lived in Boston's Back Bay and had been known to be a wealthy woman. Stupidity wasn't one of Emilia Brewster's traits and Emlen didn't think the story remotely plausible. Add to that the fact her grandmother was killed the same night she and Cullen were attacked.

Well, there were holes in that story big enough to drive an eighteen-wheeler through. The table jostled, pulling her out of her thoughts and lifting her gaze to the man sitting down across from her. Dark hair curled against his collar and brilliant blue eyes shadowed from lack of sleep and worry stared across the table at her. It was his smile, though, that had her heart racing a little faster. "Hey Cullen," she murmured, keeping her voice low.

"Hey beautiful. You okay?" he asked, nodding as the waitress brought his coffee over and a plate with two blueberry muffins. Putting one muffin on a napkin, he slid the plate over to Em before taking a bite of his own.

"Pissed off, confused and still feeling a little hazy, to be honest," Em replied, picking up the muffin and pulling the top off, taking a bite of the bottom half.

"You can tell me what happened later. For now, can I see your purse?" Cullen asked, then brushed his fingers clean as she nodded before reaching for it. He pulled the phone, her lipstick, a compact, a debit card and a couple of folded bills out before sliding his hands around the inside of the lining. Pausing, he tugged on a bit of the lining and pulled a tiny black button free and lay it on the table.

Examining it for a moment, he picked it up and dropped it in a glass of water the waitress had left. Then he reached for her phone, popped off the case, opened the back and slid out the sim card. A moment later, the sim card joined the button in the glass of water. Tucking everything back into the purse, he looked up at Emlen. "Those aren't your clothes, are they?"

"No." Emlen replied, finishing off the muffin faster than she'd expected. "Guess I was hungrier than I thought."

Cullen took a few more bites, finishing as he rose and picked up the to-go cup. "Let's go. I have a bag in the car so you can change."

Both continued being very careful with what they said, for what were now obvious reasons, so Em just nodded. She picked up her purse and the bundle of her things from the chair before following him out. Once in his truck, she slid into the back seat and opened the bag, pulling out her own jeans and a sweatshirt. Em peeled off the borrowed clothes and dressed once more. Once fully back in her own things, she stuffed her gown, heels and the borrowed clothes into a trash bag and handed it to Cullen.

Tugging ankle boots on, she leaned forward to watch as he pulled into traffic and then paused near an alley. He jumped out, dropped the trash bag into a dumpster, then got back in and pulled away. Em looked behind them and spotted the guards from the coffee shop in a black sedan a couple of car lengths back before turning forward as Cullen headed out of the city.

"I had a feeling they'd let me go too easily. I should've checked sooner. I'm sorry."

"They drugged you, didn't they?" Cullen asked, glancing in the rear-view mirror to see her face.

"Yeah, last night they put something in my tea. I woke this morning, feeling hungover. They told me I'd drank too much and passed out, but I knew that was bullshit."

A slow breath slid from him and he reached for one of her hands with his, squeezing lightly. "I'm just glad you're okay. We've been looking for you all night. One of the Garda saw you taken out of the hall with JJ and Elise and we figured you were still with them, but we weren't a hundred percent sure until you called. We couldn't get into the building to find out any details."

"Yeah, I'm fine. Just still feeling a little out of it, but it's fading fast."

"Maybe I should take you to the ER or something first?"

"And what, tell them that I was drugged by the Vice Presidential candidate, my father, after nearly being killed by my grandfather, the Federal Judge? Yeah, no. I think I'll just keep drinking water and coffee to flush it out of my system."

"Yeah, good point." Cullen fell silent while Em dozed on the ride. He nudged her awake as he pulled up to Joel's cottage. Em stretched and slid out of the truck, leaning back against it. Her gaze shifted to Cullen as he climbed out to stand beside her.

"I've been thinking. It's time we went on the offensive. I'm done being the pawn or puppet or whatever you want to call it." She turned to look out at the water, the waves rising as a storm moved closer to shore.

Cullen gave her a nod. "I agree. We need to end this once and for all."

Emlen laughed, taking his hand and leading him towards the cottage.

"End it? Oh, no. This isn't the ending. They have no idea what they've stirred up. I'm just getting started."

THE END

Want more? Pick up Revelation here! https://books2read.com/Desc2-Revelation

For nearly fifty generations, the Descendants of Charlemagne have been protected by the Garda.

Now there are only two living Descendants left - me and my father. He craves more power, and I'm trying to figure out how to access mine.

He's willing to kill to get what he wants, while I use the dead to try and stop him. Ghostly allies and magical cops aren't enough as the bodies keep piling up around me.

It's time to claim my destiny once and for all and put an end to his plans.

I'm done being played.

I'm changing the game.

24

Revelation Sample

A taste of what you'll find in the next book, Revelation!

———◇———

Emlen stood outside the mansion, back to the Charles River as she stared at the four story brick, granite and sandstone monstrosity. Em's Brewster ancestors had called the place home since the 1800's and now it belonged to her. "I can't believe my grandmother left this to me," Em said, then looked over at her companion.

His dark hair curled against his collar, bright blue eyes taking in the details before Cullen replied, "She left it to your mother and never changed her will. As Camille's only child, it came to you. Don't give the old bat credit she doesn't deserve, eh?"

"Either way, it's perfect. We needed a new base of operations and the security already in place here is excellent," Connor spoke, stepping up behind the two. Hair a shade or two lighter than his brother's, he shared Cullen's bright blue eyes but sported a crew cut for his job as a detective.

Em curled her fingers around the key fob, then pushed the wrought iron gate open. Heels clacked against the brick walkway and then granite steps wide enough for four to walk abreast. Clicking the key fob near the panel on the door released the locks and security system, allowing entry. A push of the heavy iron and oak door, and Em went inside. Marble floors in the entry, changing to polished wood throughout most of the house, gleamed under crystal and brass chandeliers. Staff had maintained the house in the months since her grandmother died. Appraisers had cataloged the items as required by the will, renovations had been done to one floor, but beyond that, no one had been here. Specifically, no family or friends.

"It smells like lemon wax," Cullen said as he wandered in and out of a couple of rooms.

"Better than smelling like old lady," Connor said.

"Connor!" Em laughed, walking past them both and down the corridor to the back of the house. The kitchen a chef's dream with a sitting area before a fireplace at one end, a round table and six chairs in a curve of windows at the other. Dropping her purse on the counter, Em opened the fridge, checked the cabinets and started to pull out items to make dinner. Groceries had been delivered earlier and stored by the staff. The cook, Mrs. Abernathy, had prepared lasagna, salad and garlic knots. All Em had to do would be heat it up, plate it up, and serve it.

The brothers unloaded the three vehicles after moving them into the underground garage and soon joined Em at the table. The three of them spent a few minutes just eating the delicious meal before Connor picked up his beer, "To next steps, new beginnings, and family."

Cullen tapped his bottle to Connor's, "To family."

Emlen smiled at them both, then added, "To next steps, new beginnings, family, and kicking ass."

"Yeah, to kicking ass," Connor laughed as Em's glass tapped their bottles. "Speaking of asses, have you heard from JJ lately?"

Em made a rude sound as she stuffed a garlic knot into her mouth and chewed.

"He calls two to three times a week and sends multiple invitations to events, etcetera, but she's refused to speak to or see him," Cullen said. "He seems to think drugging his daughter and trying to control her life is something she'll just get over."

"He's a power-hungry asshole," Emlen said as she got up to pour more wine. "You'd think being elected Vice-President would be enough to keep him busy, but noooo, he has to try fucking with my life."

"Why don't you just block his number?" Connor asked.

"Because it doesn't seem to stop him. He just sends one of his Secret Service guys to deliver a message in person. After four rounds of blocking, we've given up," Cullen replied. "It's as if there's still a tracker somewhere, but we've scanned everything. Nothing makes sense."

Emlen leaned back with her wine, sipping as she stared into the back garden patio.

"Micah, Jase, Kian, and Gina have settled in the downstairs rooms. They will be rotating shifts and filling in with other Garda as needed. Is there anything we need and haven't handled?" Cullen asked.

"Still waiting on delivery of the satellite phones. They're due in a couple of days," Connor spoke as he rose to clear the table.

"Can we keep Mrs. Abernathy as the cook?" Cullen asked as he helped clean up. "That tasted fantastic."

"Mrs. A has been a personal favorite since I have been a kid. She is happy to stay on as long as we have help for her. She's getting up there in years." Em drained her glass, handing it to Cullen to put into the dishwasher.

"What about Corinne and the twins? You going to let them come pick out stuff?" Cullen wiped his hands dry, stepping closer to tug her against his body. "How about tomorrow we can go room to room and box up what you don't want, stack it in the storage room. They can go through the boxes in storage and that's it." Em's aunt and cousins had been a royal pain in the ass about the will.

"That should shut them up for a bit, eh? Yeah, let's do that. Nothing really valuable though. If we don't like it, it can go in the attic. The Ice Bitch doesn't get a fucking thing I don't want her to have." She spoke into Cullen's chest but they all heard her words.

Sliding his hand up and down her back, Cullen comforted Em. "You hold all the cards this time, Em. And you have us and the rest of the Garda behind you. It'll be fine."

Emlen could remember the years her aunt had been her legal guardian. The loveless existence spent at boarding schools or in psychiatric offices left her with little affection for her mother's sister. "What a fucked up family, huh?" Pulling back, she gave Cullen a wan smile. "I'm going to go soak in the tub then go to bed. It's been a long day."

Cullen kissed her brow. "G'night love. Rest well. I'm just down the hall if you need me."

Connor wiped his hands dry, nodding to her, "Goodnight sis."

———————◆———————

Get Revelation here or at your favorite online shop! https://books2read.com/Desc2-Revelation

About the Author

T.K. Eldridge retired from a career in Intelligence for the US Gov't to write. The experiences from then are now being used to feed the muse for paranormal romance, mysteries, supernatural, and urban fantasy stories. When they're not writing, they are enjoying life in the Blue Ridge mountains of western North Carolina. Two dogs, a garden, a craft hobby and a love of Celtic Traditional music keep them from spending too much time at the computer.

You can connect with them on:

https://tkeldridge.com

https://twitter.com/eldridge_tk

https://www.facebook.com/groups/EldridgeEnthusiasts

https://tkeldridge.com/newsletter

Made in the USA
Las Vegas, NV
10 November 2021